THE GIRLFRIEND'S SECRET

BOOKS BY DANIEL HURST

The Holiday Home

The Couple's Revenge

The Family Trip

The Husband

The Baby Swap

The Couple Before Us

The Ex Who Came Back

Our Perfect Holiday

The Other Patient

The Doctor's Wife series

The Doctor's Wife

The Doctor's Widow

The Doctor's Mistress

The Doctor's Child

The Doctor

The Perfect Nurse series

The Perfect Nurse

The Nurse's Lie

The Nurse's Mistake

The Hunt Family series

I Want Your Family

I Stole Your Family

The Happy Family

THE GIRLFRIEND'S SECRET

DANIEL HURST

bookouture

Published by Bookouture in 2026

An imprint of Storyfire Ltd.
Carmelite House
50 Victoria Embankment
London EC4Y 0DZ

www.bookouture.com

The authorised representative in the EEA is Hachette Ireland
8 Castlecourt Centre
Dublin 15 D15 XTP3
Ireland
(email: info@hbgi.ie)

ISBN: 978-1-80550-940-0
eBook ISBN: 978-1-80550-939-4

PROLOGUE

The lifeless body at the bottom of the stairs had only been seen by one person so far.

The person who was currently standing over it.

The person who had caused it.

As the body grew colder, the life it had once held now gone, the person shifted their weight slightly. They were a little uneasy, and not just because they had taken a life. It was because they were now figuring out how they were going to get away with it.

They had a plan, but that had seemed easier before the crime had taken place.

But it was too late to go back now. The woman lying at the bottom of the stairs was already dead. Now all that was left to do for the killer was to leave and try and get away with it.

It was possible.

It could be so easy.

If only somebody else hadn't arrived at the house in that moment.

An extra person at the crime scene.

A witness.
A problem...

AFTER

ONE

LIANE

I always knew this day would come. Like anyone, I had been fearing the loss of my beloved mother. Now it is here and despite predicting, imagining and fearing such a scenario, I feel totally unprepared for it.

My dear mum is lying in that casket that is about to be carried into the church. My dear mum, who was seventy-five years old, but who potentially had many more healthy years ahead of her. My dear mum, who helped to forge me into the fifty-year-old woman I am today.

My dear mum, Valerie.

If the sight of her casket approaching wasn't already enough to set me off crying, the sight of some of the men carrying it into the church does the rest. There are six pallbearers here today, six males with the heavy coffin resting on their shoulders as they move slowly towards the gathered mourners seated in this church where I got married almost thirty years ago. On that day, my mum was seated in here and she was the one dabbing at her eyes with a tissue. But now that is me, and this is her last journey before she goes into her grave. Therefore, this is the last chance I will get to say my goodbyes.

I find myself twirling my hair, a habit I've had for as long as I can remember. I do it at times of stress, if I'm feeling awkward or anxious or afraid. It's no surprise I'm doing it now, wrapping an index finger around a long strand of my dark hair and curling it several times before finally letting go. But it won't be long until I do the same thing again.

As I watch the pallbearers approach, their steps slow and steady, oozing respect for the proud life of the woman they now carry to her final resting place, I admire each and every one of them. I admire three of the men whom I recognise from my mum's social club. Just three of her many friends, and they were happy to volunteer to help today in any way they could. But it's the other three men who carry the coffin who are causing me to cry even more than I already was.

I see my husband, Frederik, the silver hair on his head bowed but his right shoulder strong as the coffin edge rests on it. He's of Nordic origin, even though he was born and raised here in England, and he certainly possesses the strength of some of his Viking forefathers. Behind him comes my eldest son, Scott, his burly frame more down to a decade of manual labour than an ancestry from Scandinavian parts, although there will be some of his father's DNA contributing to his broad shoulders. Last, but not least, behind him is my youngest son, Joel, a much skinnier soul and that can be attributed to the fact that he has just returned from backpacking in Australia, where food was clearly neglected in favour of alcohol. I have barely seen him in the past year due to his travelling exploits on the other side of the world, but he is back now, more tanned than when he left our home in the north-west of England twelve months ago. And he looks just as upset as I am.

Bless my baby. Okay, so he's twenty-five, but he will always be my baby, just like his twenty-eight-year-old brother will be. Scott and Joel loved their grandmother, but Joel was especially close to her, and I have no doubts that he assumed she would still be alive and well when he returned from his travels. There is no way he thought he was saying a permanent goodbye to her when we all stood at the airport and wished him well before he strode away with nothing but his backpack on his shoulders and dreams of sandy beaches in his head. He planned to be away for a year or two, but he also planned to return to regale us all with tales of his adventures, and Valerie should still have been alive to hear them. But she is gone and he never got to say goodbye. None of us did. Not after she died so suddenly. My mother's death wasn't a long, drawn-out one. There were no bedside chats on a hospital ward. No dark, dreary days and long, lonely nights spent hoping for a miracle cure to whatever illness was slowly consuming her. Neither was there time to gather the family around her and have everybody say whatever they needed to say before her eyes closed and she took her last breath.

There was nothing but a sharp suddenness to the way my mother's life ended.

She fell down the stairs at home and, as I explained to the police whilst in the throes of sadness and shock, she was only found when I went to see her on a Tuesday morning like I always did. By then, it was clear it was already too late. She had lost her life, and I had lost my mother.

As the coffin creeps past the pews and several mourners bow their heads in respect as it goes, I notice one person who doesn't make a move. One person whose head remains upright. One person who is staring at the coffin just as hard as I was a moment ago.

Her name is Haven and, just like my son, she is looking tanned and slim. That's because she has come back from Australia, the same place where my son was.

She came back with him.

As the coffin reaches the front of the church and comes to rest beside where the celebrant prepares to officially begin the ceremony with a few carefully chosen words, I can't stop looking at her. This stranger to me, seated only a few spaces away from me, right at the front, with my family. It was my son's wish that she sit amongst us all and I couldn't say no to that. But I'd have preferred to keep this section of the church for close relatives who had actually *met* my dearly departed mother. Yet here she is. This young woman, only twenty-five years of age and sticking out like a sore thumb amongst this sea of older, wrinkled faces. The pews are a sea of black, as they should be because everyone knows to wear only one colour on an occasion like this. Yet she is not dressed in black. Her attire, from the dress to the cardigan to the heels. None of it is black.

It's dark blue.

Not black.

How dare she turn up here in anything other than the official, universally accepted colour for a funeral? How dare she stand out amongst everybody else here, particularly when she is the only one at the service who never met my mother before her death. How dare she do this? Where is the respect? Where is the acknowledgement? Where is the pain on her face? Joel tried to excuse her by saying she doesn't own any black clothes and in the rush for them both to fly home, there was no time to shop for a more suitable outfit.

I don't know if I believe that.

There are shops at airports, aren't there?

But I shouldn't be surprised. How can this young woman be grieving for the loss of an older woman she had never known? My dear mother, Valerie, had not touched her life in the way she had touched everybody else's here. No, the only reason Haven is in this church right now is because she is my youngest son's new girlfriend.

Joel met Haven in Australia, on Bondi Beach apparently, which sounds very glamorous. The photos of them under sunny skies Down Under certainly looked glamorous, especially when contrasted to the grey English sky that I was viewing them beneath. As I watched from afar, eagerly checking social media to see if my adventurous son had updated his account with more photos of his travels, the few images I saw told me that he and Haven were getting closer. His messages to me and his father also indicated that. He told us about her. Said he had met a great girl, told us her name and how they were spending a lot of time together. It sounded like it was going well.

At first, I wondered if Haven was Australian and feared for a moment that my son would marry her, gain residency in that far-flung country and then never come home. Such a thought might have been selfish of me, especially if he was happy, but I am a mother and I love my child, so of course I'll always be happy when my offspring are near to me as opposed to being far away. But then he told us that she was English and originated from a town only an hour away from ours and I have to say I breathed a sigh of relief.

I hoped that my baby would return to UK shores after his adventures, so that he'd be closer to me again. I prayed that I wouldn't lose him to Sydney's sandy shores and skin-soothing sunshine.

Then I got my wish. He has come home and it is far sooner than I ever expected him to. But I never wanted him to come back in these circumstances. I didn't want it to be like this. So sudden. So shocking. So sad. I didn't want him to have never said goodbye to his dear grandmother.

Nor did I want this to be the way in which I first met Haven.

We should have met differently. In more pleasant circumstances. Either her and my son returning triumphant from their time overseas and entering my house with smiles on their faces or me and my husband jetting out to Australia to see them first.

Frederik and I had already discussed taking a trip to see how our son was living over there and the fact that we could enjoy their summer while skipping some of our winter was just an added bonus. But neither of those things happened. As it was, it was down to Frederik to make a very difficult phone call to our youngest son to break the news that his grandmother had passed away.

We had no doubt that Joel would want to jump on a plane and make it back here to say his goodbyes to the sweet woman who had fed him buns and biscuits as a young boy. The only thing we doubted was whether Haven would be with him.

We assumed she might stay in Australia and wait for Joel to return to her there. After all, she couldn't be expected to attend a funeral of someone she had never met, as well as meet her boyfriend's family in such difficult circumstances.

But here she is.

Now, as the funeral gets under way and the pallbearers take their seats, I notice one other thing about this woman dressed in blue amongst a sea of black.

I notice that she is looking at me.

And then I notice that she is smiling.

TWO

LIANE

I've always liked entertaining. I've always enjoyed the opportunity to host people in my home. It might not be the biggest home in the world, but it has enough space to welcome a number of guests inside of it. And that's what is happening right now.

I decided to host the wake at my home after my mother's funeral, preferring a more personal space rather than some local pub or social club. I decided to do it here, surrounded by family photos which feature my mother. So here we all are, all thirty-three mourners from the church who witnessed the sombre but stylish send-off for Valerie, now nibbling on homemade sandwiches and cake and sipping soft drinks or something stronger from plastic cups bought from the local supermarket. Thankfully it's a sunny autumn day, so we have been able to open the patio doors and allow our guests to spill out into the back garden, reducing the 'cramped confines' feeling that could easily have overcome this occasion. But there's a chill in the air, so I doubt anyone will stay outside for long. Or maybe the chill is coming from somewhere else.

My sense of loss, perhaps.

Or my sense that something is off with my son's girlfriend.

'My deepest condolences,' says a sorrowful woman in her seventies who has approached me to shake my hand and offer her sympathies. 'Your mother was a wonderful woman. Truly wonderful. We were friends from the bowls club, and she helped me through a difficult time when my husband passed. I am sorry she is gone and I will miss her dearly.'

'Thank you so much,' I say in reply, accepting the condolences with the good grace that they were offered to me. 'I really appreciate that.'

As the woman nods her head ruefully before moving on, I am quickly into another handshake, this time with the president of the chess club that formed just one part of my mother's surprisingly large social circle. I knew Mum had a lot of friends and plenty to keep her occupied outside of her family but today has shown me just how beloved she was and just how many lives she had touched beyond those of me and our family members. It's a pleasure to see all these people, but it's also a sad sight, because the more mourners there are at a funeral, the more sadness there is in a community. Trying to cheer all these people up with a few platefuls of hastily made sandwiches and big bowls of crisps suddenly seems so futile.

'Thank you,' I say to the chess president before he moves over to pick up a soft drink from the side table while I turn and accept a hug from my dear husband.

'You're doing so well,' Frederik says as he gives me a tight squeeze, and it's as if he knew the exact moment when I needed something stronger than just a handshake and a few kind words. I needed companionship, real physical intimacy, and here is my husband right on hand to provide me with it. This is just one of the many reasons why I love him so much. He always knows what's best for me and, right now, I need him holding me up before I collapse from trying to put on a brave face in front of all these people.

'Have you had something to eat? Can I get you a drink?' Frederik asks, concerned that in amongst all the welcoming of well-wishers in my home, I have forgotten to give myself some sustenance to help fuel me through this difficult day. He would be right because I haven't taken a bite of a sandwich since we got back here, nor have I had the smallest sip of water either. The truth is, I lost my appetite when I lost my mother and while I know I need to eat to stay strong, it's easier said than done. At least grief might help me lose a little weight and that can't be a bad thing. I don't think I'll ever return to the slim days of my twenties, but losing a few pounds as I enter my fifties can't hurt. And then, as if to emphasise that thought currently running through my head, I catch sight of Haven at the buffet table, stuffing a ham and cheese sandwich into her face before pouring herself a glass of red wine from one of the bottles Frederik had set out before we left for the church.

As I watch my son's girlfriend, it's as if she is totally oblivious to the sorrow that surrounds her. Rather than demonstrate slow and thoughtful movements, aware that she is in an uncomfortable environment with people who are grieving deeply, she is acting as if she is at an all-inclusive hotel and can't wait to gorge herself on whatever she can get her hands on. As she sticks another sandwich in her mouth, I have no idea how she maintains such a slender figure, before remembering how I could eat anything I wanted at that age too and it didn't seem to make a difference. She'll realise that such luck runs out one day, but for now, she is fully in her era of calorific consumption, and she doesn't seem to care who sees it.

If I'm honest, my reason for watching her with increasing levels of disdain is less about how much she is eating and more about how she smiled at me back in the church. It was such a strange thing to do in that moment as tears rolled down my cheeks and the pallbearers had just placed down the coffin. Why smile? Why not just look at me and offer something else, like a look of pure compassion or sympathy? I'd have even understood if she had quickly averted her eyes from mine due to the awkwardness. But to smile suggests she wasn't feeling awkward in that moment at all. It also suggests she wasn't even feeling sad. But how can someone not be sad at a funeral? The occasion demands it. Any happiness is left at the church door and not regained again until hours, days or maybe even months later. But not so for Haven. Not so for this woman who has infiltrated my family and who might be here to stay depending on how things go between her and my youngest son.

I see Joel then, watching as he sidles up to Haven, sliding an arm around her impossibly slim waist before giving her a kiss on the cheek. It's sweet of my son to be checking on his girlfriend, especially here where she doesn't know anyone anywhere near as well as him, and Haven turns to acknowledge the gesture. But she doesn't just smile like she did to me at the church, nor does she stop chewing on her latest sandwich. Instead, she opens her mouth and pulls a funny face, not unlike a young child who is messing around at the dinner table in front of their parents.

It's an immature move, but my son responds with a small laugh. Perhaps it was just an awkward reaction on his part, or maybe he did actually find it funny, despite the circumstances. Lord knows he could use a little levity at a time like this. But whatever the effect of the silly facial expression, it's another example of how Haven seems totally nonplussed about being here, in my home, at my mother's funeral, and surrounded by her boyfriend's family, whom she barely knows.

If I had met Frederik's family like this, I'd have been on my best behaviour. It would have been all 'pleases and thank yous', but mostly I would have kept myself to myself. Fortunately, I never had to experience this because I met Frederik's family in much brighter circumstances, accompanying my man as we met his parents for a meal in town one Saturday night. Sure, it was still nerve-wracking, but it was better than meeting them after somebody had just died. I had initially felt sorry for Haven and how her first time around us would be under these unfortunate circumstances. But the more I watch her, the more I see she doesn't seem to need anybody to feel sorry for her.

'I just can't believe it,' comes the female voice nearby, and I turn to see one of my mother's best friends, Ruth, lingering to my left. 'Val was so fit and active. I just don't understand how she could have fallen down the stairs. She'd never been the type to be unsteady on her feet.'

'Unfortunately, it could have just been age catching up with her,' Frederik says with a sad shake of the head. 'Or perhaps a simple accident. I suppose we've all been guilty of almost toppling down the stairs at one time or another, no matter how old we are. I know I've almost lost my footing a few times myself.'

'But Val was always so careful. I can't believe she could just slip and fall like that,' Ruth replies ruefully. 'Was it definitely an accident?'

'Of course it was. The police have no reason to think otherwise,' Frederik replies quickly.

'But could it have been something other than her just falling?' Ruth asks.

'Like what?' Frederik asks.

'I don't know,' Ruth says. 'I just can't envision Val ever being weak and vulnerable, I suppose.'

'Me neither,' I add before the memory of seeing Mum at the bottom of the stairs flashes before my eyes again and I have to turn away as the tears take hold.

As I hear Frederik accept some condolences from Ruth, I rush to find the nearest tissue box. But on the way, I hear something that makes me stop still.

It's her. Haven. She's talking to an elderly man by the buffet table.

And what she says turns my blood cold.

'Accidents are awful, but they happen all the time. At least she didn't suffer. At least it was over quickly for her.'

I stare at Haven and wonder how she could say such a thing. How does she know my mother didn't suffer? How does she know she wasn't lying in pain for several agonising minutes or even hours before she passed? How does she know even the slightest thing about what happened?

Then I see it again. It's not directed at me this time, but I still see it.

That same smile.

Out of all the people in my house right now, only one of them seems happy.

Her.

THREE

LIANE

Most of the mourners have now left my house, but my home is far from empty. That's because my husband is here, as are my two sons. After a long day, it's finally time for family. Well, almost. There is still one person here who isn't technically family.

Haven.

'What a lovely send-off she had,' Haven says as she joins Joel on the sofa with yet another glass of wine. *How many has she had now?* 'I thought the funeral was really sweet and it was nice to see how many friends she had.'

I'm not sure I'd ever describe a funeral as sweet. Such a word is usually reserved for occasions like christenings, weddings or surprise birthday parties. Yet here is Haven talking about my mum's funeral as if it was something to be savoured rather than survived.

'I never knew she was so popular,' Joel says. 'But I guess that was Grandma. Always full of surprises.'

'Like what?' Haven asks, intrigued to learn more, though I wish she'd just shut up and be quiet at this point because her youthful exuberance feels very out of place on a day like this.

'Remember the time she told us she had done a bungee jump in Canada,' Scott says from the sofa where he reclines horizontally, and I can't help but smile at my eldest son for reminding us of that memory.

'Yeah, she had kept that one quiet,' I say. 'I think we were all shocked when she got home and showed us the video.'

'Your granny did a bungee jump?' Haven asks Joel, looking stunned. 'How old was she at the time?'

'In her sixties,' my youngest replies, much to Haven's astonishment.

'Wow, she sounds like so much fun. I wish I had met her! I wanted to do a bungee jump in Australia, but I chickened out at the last minute. Remember?'

'I do,' Joel says. 'I guess my grandma was braver than you.'

Haven jabs Joel in the ribs playfully before snuggling into his shoulder, and while I would usually be happy to see my son so loved up with someone, I can't shake the feeling that something is off with Haven. I've felt it ever since I first met her, which was yesterday, just after her and my son had got off their flight.

'There he is,' Frederik had said when he'd spotted our youngest son with his backpack on his shoulders, appearing beneath the Arrivals sign looking far more tanned than he had twelve months earlier.

'And there she is,' I had added as I saw the woman he was walking beside, a backpack on her shoulders too and an even deeper tan than the one my son was sporting.

She was very attractive, a fact I had picked up from the photos of her my son had shared online, but she looked even more stunning in real life. I hadn't looked half as good as her when I was in my mid-twenties, but then again, I hadn't been free to keep fit, travel the world and follow every one of my whims. I was already on baby number two by then.

'The traveller returns!' Frederik cried as our son

approached before I opened my arms wide to welcome my son back to his homeland.

'Hey, guys,' Joel said before I enveloped him in a huge hug, the hug I had been impatiently waiting to give him for the past year.

'Oh, I've missed you,' I whispered to him, before noticing he felt a little skinnier than when he had left and making a mental note to feed him up for as long as he was back here. He hadn't yet said how long he planned to be home, and we hadn't pressed him on the subject. He was only back because of his grandma's funeral, so I felt it best to get through that before discussing what his plans were for the future.

'Come here, son,' Frederik said before giving his boy a big hug too.

'Hi, I'm Haven,' the young woman standing beside our tightly squeezed son said then, and I made sure to open my arms wide to give her a big welcome too. This was my first impression, and I wanted it to be a good one. There's nothing worse than a girlfriend not liking their partner's mother, and I definitely didn't want that, so I was making an extra effort. I just want my son to be happy, and I hope he always will be. But wanting your child to be happy 24/7 is a futile wish because it's impossible. You can protect them from everything, except themselves.

'It's so lovely to meet you,' I said as we embraced, slightly tentatively, but that was only natural.

'You too,' Haven said. 'And I'm so sorry to hear about your mum. She sounded like a wonderful woman.'

'Thank you,' I replied, touched at the sentiment, and as Frederik greeted Haven, I felt like things were off to a good start, or at least as good as they could be given the circumstances.

Things seemed okay as we drove back from the airport too, Frederik and I in the front of the car while Joel and Haven sat in the back and regaled us with a few stories from their long trip back from Australia. Hearing their two young voices, each of them at a stage in life where they still had so much ahead of them, contrasted greatly with how I felt having just lost Mum and feeling like a huge part of my life was already over. But I was happy that Joel seemed less upset than I feared he might be, although I always knew my youngest son tended to hide his true feelings behind laughter and jokes. Scott is the one who lets everyone know how he feels at all times, be it good or bad, whereas Joel is more introverted and more likely to hide parts of himself, especially vulnerable parts like sadness, behind smiles and sarcasm. But it was good to have my son home, if only for a short while, and I knew all of us being back together would help us heal quicker from the hole my mother had left in our family.

It's strange, but as I sit here now, after the funeral and the wake, I feel totally different about things. Sure, it's still nice to have my two children here, but it's not the same. Not with Haven here too. Not with how I have felt the longer I have been around her. Not with how I can't shake the indiscernible feeling that there is something very off about her.

As I watch her pick up her phone and use Face ID to unlock it before her fingers start scrolling across the screen, my family offers a welcome distraction from my paranoia.

'So, what's your plans now, bro?' Scott asks his sibling as Frederik hands me a cup of tea and takes a seat beside me. 'Back to Australia or heading somewhere else to avoid getting a proper job like the rest of us?'

Joel rolls his eyes at his brother's sarcastic jibe before firing back one of his own.

'Sorry for not living the dream in a mechanic's garage like you do all day,' he says with a cheeky smirk.

'I own that mechanic's garage, so I am living my dream, actually,' Scott snaps back, unable to hide his annoyance at his little brother's dismissal of his life choices.

'Yeah, oil-soaked rags and broken-down cars sound so much better than sunbathing on Bondi and watching the sun set behind the Opera House,' Joel says before Scott picks up a sofa cushion and launches it at his brother's head, laughing.

'Boy, we haven't missed this,' Frederik says with a chuckle, even though I know he has missed it just as much as me. It's clear that Scott and Joel have missed it too, despite what they might say to each other, and for another brief moment, it's lovely to have us all back under one roof. And then I get a reminder that there is another person with us.

'We're actually thinking of staying in England,' Haven says, and such is my shock at what I've just heard, I almost spill my tea.

'Really?' I ask, looking from her to Joel.

'Erm, yeah, I think so,' Joel replies, seeming a little less certain of that than his girlfriend, although he isn't dispelling the idea either.

'So the dream life in Australia isn't actually any better than working in a mechanic's garage back here in this rainy town, is it?' Scott says with a laugh.

'Shut up,' Joel says, returning the cushion at his brother's head with just as much force as it was thrown at him a few moments earlier.

'Are you serious? You're not going back to travelling?' I ask, wanting to firm up the facts here in amongst all the sibling shenanigans going on.

'Yeah, we've talked about it, but we think we might stay and get a place together here,' Haven replies.

'That's wonderful,' Frederik says. 'You mean I won't get any more phone calls in the middle of the night from my son asking me to transfer him a few hundred pounds because he's spent it all on partying again?'

Everyone laughs at my husband's comment, simply because

we all know it to be true. There have certainly been a few times this year when Joel has completely forgotten the time difference between the UK and Australia and phoned home to request some emergency funds to keep his fun in Australia alive. There's nothing that proves you never stop being a parent more than a 2 a.m. call from your penniless, hungover and charming child of twenty-five, asking for an urgent bank transfer to get him through the day Down Under while your day hasn't even started yet.

'I guess not,' Joel says. 'Sorry to disappoint you.'

We all laugh again and, just as I thought, having Joel home is helping take my mind off my mother's untimely demise, for now, at least.

'But how will you get your own place if you have no money?' Scott asks. 'No offence, but aren't you just a couple of broke backpackers?'

'Charming,' Haven says, looking a little aggrieved by how my eldest has just summed up her and her boyfriend's lives.

I notice Scott doesn't look particularly amused either, so I guess he wasn't exactly joking there. That makes me wonder if I am not the only one who has some misgivings about Haven. But there's no time to dwell on it. Not when my youngest son suddenly speaks up.

'We were wondering,' Joel says as he looks at me and then his father, 'would it be okay if Haven and I moved in here for a while, just until we save some money and figure out where we are going to live?'

I barely even need to think about it. There's no way I am going to say no to my son moving back home, especially not when the alternative is him going back to the other side of the world. But I do hesitate, just for the smallest of seconds, and it's because of the person sitting on the sofa next to him. The person who now comes as a package with my son and the person who will also be living here if Joel comes back home.

Can I have Haven in my home full-time, for however long that might be?

I guess I have no choice. Neither does my husband, and the subtle but knowing nod we share with one another confirms it.

'Yes, of course,' I say with a smile, and Joel looks pleased to hear that. But then I notice something strange.

For the first time all day, Haven seems to have stopped smiling.

FOUR

LIANE

'She's lovely, isn't she?' Frederik says as he takes off his watch and places it on the bedside table. 'And she seems to make Joel very happy.'

'Yeah,' I mumble back as I take off my earrings and put them back in the top drawer of my dressing table. I haven't worn earrings for a while because I haven't had many occasions to wear them. I only got them out for the funeral, so now they can go away again, and I hope that is the last funeral I go to for a very long time.

'I can't believe they're not going back to Australia,' Frederik says then as he takes off his shirt and reveals the still impressive, but slowly declining physique of a man who used to swim and stretch often but now barely has time for that with his demanding day job in the local council office. He still has muscles, but they're more naturally gifted than those that have been honed in the gym. I know Frederik wishes he had more time for working out, but that wouldn't help pay the bills, and we have plenty of those. They promise to be even bigger bills soon, now that my son and his girlfriend will be using the facilities around here.

I work as a cleaner, though I am currently on compassionate leave after informing my employer about the loss of my mother. What I haven't informed them of yet is that I do not plan to return to work. I haven't informed my husband of that plan either, but I will do very soon.

'I thought Joel was loving it over there,' my husband goes on. 'I'm surprised he'd give all that up to come back here.'

'It's good that he wants to come home,' I say as I take off my dress, doing so in such a fashion as to not give my husband too much of a glimpse of my body, because like him I have lost my shape over the years but, unlike him, I am more self-conscious about it.

'Yeah, of course it is. I'm just saying that it's a surprise, that's all. At his age, he could be doing anything, yet he's moving back in here with us.'

'We were married with two children at his age,' I remind my husband. 'Maybe he's got the travelling out of his system and wants to settle down like we did.'

'Yeah, except we settled down before we had travelled,' Frederik reminds me rather unnecessarily.

'What do you mean by that?'

'I'm just saying I hope he's really ready to be back here. To get a job. To save up money and get a proper place to live. I hope he doesn't regret it because it won't be easy for him being cooped up with Mum and Dad again 24/7 after being away for so long.'

'It'll be fine,' I say, though I have no concrete evidence to base that opinion on. Rather, it's just hope that my son will love being back home and not quickly resent that he has swapped sunsets in Sydney for boxsets on the sofa with his parents.

'Maybe it will be,' Frederik says as he puts on a pair of old shorts before getting beneath the duvet. 'Maybe he is really ready to settle down and do the things we were doing at his age. Maybe Haven is the mother of our future grandkids.'

That sudden sentence causes me to forget that I was making an effort to shield my body from my husband, and I turn around to look at him as he lies in our bed.

'That's rushing things, don't you think?' I say. 'They've only been together a few months.'

'Yes, but they seem very happy,' Frederik replies, his eyes locked on mine rather than flitting down my semi-naked body, and I'm not sure if I should be relieved at that or dismayed.

'I know they do. I'm just saying that it's very early days and sitting on a beach all day in Australia is very different to living in the real world back here, so let's see how they manage with a little more routine in their lives,' I reply before covering up the parts of my skin that were on show with an oversized T-shirt that I have taken to sleeping in over the past few years.

Lingerie is long gone from this house.

'Of course,' Frederik says as he picks up the crime thriller from his bedside table and thumbs through the pages to find where he is up to in the story. One of my husband's many follies is that he doesn't use bookmarks, a fact I find bizarre, but we're all different in some way, aren't we?

'What do you think of her?' I ask him before he can start reading, assuming he has found the correct page given his disregard for precise tracking.

'Huh?' Frederik says, still flicking through the pages and possibly having some difficulty finding the right place in the book to resume reading, not that he would ever admit to it this far into our marriage.

'What do you think about Haven?' I ask, keen to get his honest assessment of his son's girlfriend in the sanctuary of our bedroom where no one else has to hear our thoughts. Sure, Joel and Haven might be sleeping in his old bedroom down the hallway right now, but they can't hear any discussion in here. Not unless they put their ears to the door and listen in, but why would they do that?

Just to make sure, before Frederik can answer me, I open our bedroom door to check that no one is out there. It's all clear.

'She's very friendly,' Frederik says as I quickly close the door again. 'Confident too. I haven't sensed any awkwardness from her since she has been here.'

'Neither have I,' I say. 'But isn't that weird? I mean, shouldn't there be at least some awkwardness on her part?'

'Would you prefer there to be?' Frederik asks with a laugh, looking up from the book that he may or may not have found the right page to read from.

'No, I'm just saying, it is a little strange how relaxed she has seemed since she got here. Like at the wake today, I noticed she was talking to lots of different people. It was as if she was at a cocktail party with friends, not surrounded by strangers at a very depressing event following the death of someone she had never met.'

'You'd rather she sat in a corner and didn't talk to anybody?' my husband says with his annoying tendency for sarcasm.

I answer that by rolling my eyes before I get into bed alongside him.

'I think her confidence can only be a good thing, especially for Joel,' Frederik says. 'We both know he could use a little confidence boost himself every now and again, so maybe she can help with that.'

'Maybe,' I say. 'Or maybe she is a little overconfident.'

'How so?'

'I don't know. I'm just getting a weird vibe from her.'

'A vibe. You do realise you're fifty years old. I'm not sure you can get away with words like vibe anymore.'

'Oh shut up,' I say, slapping my husband's shoulders, playfully, but just hard enough so he knows not to make comments about my advancing age again anytime soon. It's not as if he isn't exactly the same age as me either, although to be fair, I don't ever remember him uttering the 'vibe' word before. I don't think

I've said it before either, but it's the best way I could think of to describe how I feel around Haven. It is a vibe and it is an increasingly uncomfortable one. I wish it wasn't so because I want my son to be happy. Any mother would.

So why do I feel unhappy?

It could just be about Mum. As Frederik puts down his book, he seems to think so too.

'It's been a hard time, and you got a hell of a shock when you found your mother,' my husband says, taking hold of my hand. 'You need to just focus on taking time for yourself and not worrying about other people. I know that seems impossible for you because you're so selfless, but you need to try. I'm here to support you. Okay?'

I relax as Frederik's words of encouragement wash over me, a needed reminder that I have been operating under a heightened state of stress recently and, therefore, anything I think or feel comes with a big asterisk because this is not my normal state. I guess that extends to how I feel about my son's new girlfriend too, and maybe now they are living with us, I will realise that Haven is nothing but good news and could be a very welcome addition to our family.

As Frederik returns to his book, I think about rolling over and getting some sleep. Lord knows I will be glad when this day is over. You only bury your mother once in your lifetime, but once is more than enough. But before I can try and sleep, I realise I've forgotten to bring a glass of water up and, knowing how thirsty I often feel if I wake in the night, I decide that I'd better go and get one, just in case.

* * *

I get out of bed and leave my husband engrossed in his book, creeping down the hallway past my youngest son's bedroom. It's a room that has been empty for over a year but is now occupied.

My little boy is in there again, although I would never verbally call him my little boy because at twenty-five, he would be more prone to teasing me if I said such a thing. I also think about how he is not alone in his room because Haven is in there with him.

It's funny, but it was only a few minutes ago that I was wondering if somebody could be eavesdropping on my conversation on the other side of the bedroom door. Yet now, I realise I am in a position to do exactly that to somebody else's conversation.

But I shouldn't do it. I should just move on to go and get my drink from the kitchen before returning to bed. So why do I linger in the hallway? Why do I move my head closer to my son's bedroom door? Why am I now trying to hear if anything is being said on the other side of it?

I just want the best for him.

But am I behaving in the best way to get that?

It doesn't take long for me to detect that words are being spoken.

I can hear Haven talking. It's a soft voice, but it's audible.

What is she saying?

It could be nothing. Some anecdote from her past, or from travelling, or a simple comment about plans for tomorrow. But it's none of those things. Instead, she is talking about me.

'I don't think your mother likes me very much,' I hear Haven saying to Joel. 'And I'm not sure I like her either.'

FIVE

LIANE

It was hard to sleep with Haven's words ringing in my ears. Okay, so I shouldn't have been eavesdropping on a private conversation but, then again, it was a conversation that was occurring in my house. Maybe I had a right to hear it, and I think I did, considering I was the person being discussed.

Haven said that she thinks I don't like her and, given the vibe I have been getting from her, she might be right about that so far. But then she also said that she didn't like me, and while that could just be a natural reaction to her sensing my unease towards her, it still felt shocking to hear.

Have I been awful to her in any way? As far as I can tell, I have been nothing but welcoming. I have opened up my home to her and allowed her to stay here. Sure, I've only done that because she comes with my son, but still, I could have said no and told her to stay with her own family, whoever they are, because she hasn't opened up about them to us yet. But no, I have allowed her into my home. I also allowed her to attend my mother's funeral, to be alongside Joel on what was a difficult day and, really, just a day for close family and friends. So how can she say she doesn't like me? It could just be me being overly emotional after recent stresses and strains, or there could truly be some substance there.

I wish I had been able to hear what Joel had said in response to Haven's statement, but I couldn't. He must have been whispering and I failed to hear anything after that. Maybe they both just drifted off to sleep. Perhaps Haven was not thinking clearly, consumed by jetlag and the stress of the funeral and meeting so many strangers.

Who knows?

Not me.

All I know is I slept badly and now I am leaving my bedroom to go and make myself some breakfast. Food should cheer me up. Or at least I think it might until I enter the kitchen.

The first thing I notice is the mess.

This room was tidy before I went to bed, but as I walk in and see the surfaces, I can hardly believe my eyes. What has happened in here? There are dirty plates on the counters, half-filled cups of orange juice, and crumbs all over a chopping board. Add to that an empty packet of ham, two pieces of bread going stale on the side and two empty crisp packets and it looks like somebody had quite the feast in here.

At first, I think about my husband. He left for work about half an hour ago and usually makes his breakfast before he goes to his office. But he doesn't tend to consume ham, bread and crisps at this time of the day and, even if he did, he wouldn't leave such a mess in his wake. He is very good at tidying up after himself, so I doubt this was him. The next suspect then would be Joel, and my son has been known to go rummaging for food in the early hours of the morning while the rest of the family sleeps. But that was when he was a ravenous teenager, and even then, like his father, he always made an effort to tidy up after himself. But if it's not him then it means it must be her.

Could Haven have made all this mess? It's possible. If so, I don't object to her helping herself to some food if she was hungry, because she is a guest here and I want her to feel comfortable. But I do object to her leaving my kitchen in such a state, especially after I worked hard to get it clean and tidy again after hosting my mother's wake yesterday.

Disinfecting surfaces and sweeping the floor had been the last thing I had wanted to do after laying my mother to rest, but I had forced myself to do it, with my husband's help, because I knew it was important to keep a clean environment. It's second nature for me to reach for a dustpan and brush anyway, given my day job, but it's always been important that I make the effort as much with my home as I do with my clients'. My fragile mental state won't be helped by living in a messy home, so I made sure there was no mess. But despite that, I am now surrounded by one.

I hear footsteps coming down the stairs and realise Joel and Haven are surfacing from their slumber, and suddenly I feel like an intruder in my own home. I should be totally relaxed here, but I feel awkward as I hear them approaching. I feel how Haven should have felt when she arrived here, only she didn't feel awkward at all. Why am I now the one suffering from that feeling instead of her?

'Morning, Mum,' I hear Joel say behind me and I turn around to see my sleepy son entering the kitchen, his bleary eyes still displaying the effects of the jetlag he will be battling after such a long flight from Australia.

'Good morning,' I say before I see Haven enter the room behind him. She looks sleepy too, not that fatigue seems to have had too much of a negative effect on her appearance. She still looks good, even with bedhead, jetlag and no make-up.

'Morning, Liane,' Haven says cheerfully, the lilt of her voice catching me off guard. Maybe she didn't make this mess after all. If she did, she would surely be a little sheepish about it. Wouldn't she?

'Anyone for a cup of tea?' Joel asks as he approaches the kettle, and Haven answers in the affirmative before taking a seat at the breakfast bar that is still littered with various food and drink items. But I don't answer because I'm still trying to figure out who made this mess.

'Did either of you get up in the night?' I ask Joel as he fills the kettle with water before putting it on to boil. I'm twirling my hair again because I'm nervous about having a conversation about the mess.

'I did,' Haven replies, not even trying to deny it, which again makes me wonder why she would be so bold if she did make this mess. Surely she can see the state this kitchen is in?

'Oh, okay,' I say. 'Did you make yourself a sandwich or something?'

'Yeah, I made a snack for me and Joel,' Haven replies nonchalantly. 'We were both wide awake at 3 a.m. with jetlag, so I came down here and got us something to eat. Is that okay?'

'I told her it would be fine, Mum,' Joel replies as the kettle boils.

'Oh, yes, of course it's fine,' I say. 'It's just that, well...'

I'm not sure how to say what I want to say without coming across as a boring stickler for tidiness. But I also don't want what has happened here to go unrecognised because I don't want it to become the norm. Surely common decency and manners whilst staying in somebody else's home are a given?

'Is it about the mess?' Haven asks then, thankfully raising the subject for me.

'Yes,' I say, a little relieved that I am not the only one who has noticed all the evidence of food preparation around here.

'Sorry about that. I'll tidy it up now,' Haven says as she slides off her seat and picks up the empty crisp packets.

'No, I'll do it,' Joel says. 'I should have done it last night, but I was so sleepy.'

'Me too. It had been a long day and, with jetlag, I just wasn't thinking clearly,' Haven adds, and suddenly I feel bad for being so annoyed about this mess. An untidy kitchen is hardly the end of the world, especially given what happened yesterday, when we all attended the event that did mark the end of the world for my mother. So I should just shrug and forget about this rather than make a bigger deal out of it.

'Don't worry, I'll tidy up,' I say, trying to sound as casual as I can. 'I was just checking if it was you or my husband who had made some food in the night.'

'I see,' Haven replies with a laugh. 'Well, he's not guilty this time.'

There's that chirpy, utterly unawkward demeanour again, and as I watch Haven put some of the rubbish into the bin, I wish I possessed one ounce of the calm confidence she carries. Is it weird for a fifty-year-old woman with a husband and two healthy kids to envy someone half their age who has little else in life other than a backpack with a few belongings in it? Maybe, or maybe it's more common than I think. I might appear to have more than Haven does on the surface of things, but she clearly has something I don't.

She has freedom from overthinking every tiny little thing.

As Joel makes the tea, I help Haven tidy up, and by the time we are done, the kitchen is looking back to its best.

'So, what are your plans today?' I ask the loved-up pair who can't seem to keep their hands off one another as they sit on the opposite side of the breakfast bar to me.

'We might just rest. We're still both really tired from the flight,' Joel says, and that's understandable, so I won't try and push them to do anything productive. Like job hunt so they can earn some money to move out, for example. The truth is, it's early days, but I love having Joel back home. As for Haven, hopefully, in time, I'll be glad she is around too.

I'm just about to suggest breakfast when my phone rings and when I see who is calling me, I feel a sinking feeling in my stomach. But I have to answer it, so I do just that, although not before leaving the breakfast bar and turning away from Joel and Haven.

'Hello?' I say before I hear the voice of the solicitor in charge of settling my mother's final wishes regarding her Last Will and Testament. Her name is Jane, and my mother told me she would be the one to deal with when she was gone regarding her estate and the distribution of it to her remaining family.

'Hello, Liane. I hope you're well and the funeral service was not too difficult for you?'

'Thank you, it went as well as could be hoped for,' I say before glancing back at the breakfast bar to see that Joel is totally uninterested in my conversation and is looking at his phone instead. But Haven is watching me, so I step a little further away.

'I'm just calling to see if you are free to come for a meeting to discuss your mother's will,' Jane says. 'I appreciate if it is too early and you need a little more time, but your mother was very organised, so I am just letting you know that we can progress things whenever you are ready.'

I knew my mother was organised in regard to her finances and what might happen to them when she died because she told me so. The only thing she didn't plan for was dying before her time, but then nobody plans for that, I suppose.

'I'm ready,' I say, figuring it's a task that needs to be done, so rather sooner than later.

Jane gives me the details of when I am to meet her at her office before I thank her and end the call. When I do, I turn back and see that Joel is still engrossed in his phone. I also see that Haven has been watching me this entire time.

Does she know what that phone call was about? I have no idea. But one thing I do know is that she will not be joining me, Frederik, Scott and Joel when we go to hear how my mother has chosen to distribute the wealth she left behind.

It's strictly a matter for family and Haven is not that.

Not yet.

Maybe not ever.

SIX

LIANE

As Frederik drives me towards the address where a complete stranger will go into detail about my late mother's finances, I think about how a person ever gets into that line of work. Who wants to spend their time sifting through the wishes of the dead? It seems like quite a morbid job, a daily reminder that we all die and everything we have accumulated before that just ends up getting passed to somebody else. If anything, it might make the person doing that job wonder why they are working so hard themselves, knowing full well whatever they earn can't be taken with them to the next life.

Or maybe I'm just overthinking things again.

'I hope the boys are on time,' Frederik says as we get close to the destination on our sat-nav, and he's not the only one. I have told Scott and Joel not to be late in getting here and they both assured me that they wouldn't be.

Our eldest son will be coming straight from the mechanic's garage that he owns, taking an hour out of his busy day fixing cars to be present for this. As for Joel, he went into town to show Haven a few of the local sights before telling us that he would get a taxi to meet us here. Both our boys will no doubt stand to inherit something from my mother and it could be a fairly substantial amount given how good Mum was at squirrelling away her hard-earned cash.

After many years spent working as a PA to a wealthy banker in London, she earned a good amount of money and not all of it was spent on the large home she lived and ultimately died in. She always emphasised to me the importance of 'saving for a rainy day' and while I might not have done as well as I could have at heeding that advice at times, my mother certainly practised what she preached. Now I'm just about to find out exactly how far she took it.

As we reach the car park, I see Scott parking his own vehicle, a beaten-down pickup truck, and give him a wave before we climb out of our car. But looking around, I fail to see any sign of Joel, which is frustrating because our meeting is due to begin in two minutes.

'Let's go inside. I'm sure he'll be here in a minute,' Frederik says, and the three of us head in, my husband teasing our eldest about how he has turned up to an important meeting wearing an oil-stained sweater. But as Scott quite rightly replies, how else is a mechanic supposed to look in the middle of the working week?

'Take a seat,' a kindly receptionist says to us after we have entered the fairly plush offices, and we do just that, with me hoping that my son is not getting any oil on the fabric chair he has just sat down on. Before we can get too comfortable, an office door opens and I see a smiling brunette woman in a smart suit. She looks every bit the solicitor and despite making an effort with my own appearance for this meeting, she has surpassed me in her simple work attire.

'Hello, I'm Jane. We spoke on the phone the other day. Thank you for coming in and again, my condolences for your loss.'

Jane extends her hand for me to shake, and I do just that,

grateful for her pleasant, professional demeanour during these trying times. Jane greets Frederik and Scott too before noticing that there is one person missing from our party.

'He should be here any minute,' Frederik says, pre-empting her question about Joel's whereabouts, so that the solicitor will not need to explain to us how important it is that he does make it here. That's because the meeting can only be conducted if everyone mentioned in the will is present, to avoid any potential disputes at a later date, not that I foresee any. I have heard plenty of horror stories about families falling apart after the reading of a will. Tales of relatives who jealously contest what one another is getting and siblings sparring over who got the most from Mum or Dad and all manner of other awful examples. In this case, I feel fortunate to be an only child because I won't have to split my inheritance with a brother or sister or potentially fight over it if it isn't what either of us wanted. Things will be cleaner and simpler this way. I have a best friend who lost her sister's friendship after the pair of them fought viciously over their late father's estate, and what unfolded afterwards would have been enough to make that poor man turn in his grave.

No such dramas today, thankfully.

But there could be a drama if Joel doesn't show up.

'I'll go and check outside,' Scott says before leaving the office to go and look for any sign of his brother in the car park. As we wait, Jane invites me and Frederik into her office, and we follow her into a room that is full of mahogany furniture, leatherbound books and other things that make it clear this is the office of a legal-minded person. I doubt I could understand some of the titles of these books on the shelves, let alone any of the words written in them, so I'm glad I'm not the one who has to spend their day deciphering important documents like wills and the like. That is Jane's domain and she is ready to show us what she can do. But there are still two empty seats on our side of the desk, so she can't start yet.

I glance back towards the open doorway and when I do, I see Scott re-entering the office. He's quickly followed by Joel. That's a relief, so I turn back to Jane and smile, satisfied that my sons have successfully managed to follow orders, for today at least.

'We're all here,' I say as I wait for Scott and Joel to take their seats beside me and their father, but while Scott does, Joel remains standing. It's only when I turn back around that I see why.

He has not come alone.

Haven is here too.

That's despite me reminding him that she is not a part of this very private meeting.

'Oh, sorry. This is just for family,' I have to say to her. 'Are you okay to wait outside? This shouldn't take long,' I say, figuring that is the politest way I can deal with this awkward situation.

'It's okay, she can be here,' Joel says before he offers his girlfriend his chair and then looks around for another chair he can use as his own. He locates one in the corner of Jane's office and starts to drag it over, but before he can finish doing that, I have to stand.

'No, I'm sorry, but this really is just for family,' I say and look to Jane in the hopes that she will back me up with this. 'Isn't that right?'

'Well, yes, although she can sit in on this if you are okay with her being here,' Jane says, which doesn't actually help me because now she has put the ball back in my court.

I look to Frederik then for help and he gets the message.

'I think this is best dealt with privately,' he says. 'I hope you understand, Haven.'

'No, she stays,' Joel says, surprising me with his forcefulness.

To my dismay, Haven doesn't go anywhere.

I look at her incredulously, aghast that she has ignored both mine and my husband's wishes. What kind of person ignores the requests of her partner's polite parents? But I'm just as shocked at my son's behaviour too because he's always been so well-mannered and well-behaved and has rarely disobeyed me or his father, particularly in public settings like this one.

As Joel takes his seat, I decide this has gone far enough, so I state the obvious.

'You can't be in here, Haven, because this is a discussion about my mother's personal finances and, no offence, but you didn't even know her.'

Surely she will have got the message now. Loud and clear. Right?

'That's where you're wrong,' Haven replies to my astonishment. 'I did know your mother. In fact, I knew her quite well.'

SEVEN

LIANE

I stare at Haven with a mixture of shock and disgust. I'm shocked because she has just said that she knew my mother and I cannot see how that is even remotely possible. As for the disgust, that exists because it feels like this young woman has just said the most ludicrous thing simply to try and win a dispute that would allow her to stay in this room where she is not welcome.

Why lie about such a thing as knowing my mother when she plainly didn't?

Such is the strangeness of her statement, I'm not the only one who has been temporarily rendered speechless. That is until Frederik finds his voice.

'I beg your pardon, but how did you know Valerie?' he asks our son's girlfriend as politely as he can.

I have to give him credit for his control. I certainly would not have asked that question in such a calm manner. Then again, it's not his mother Haven is so brazenly lying about.

'It's true,' Joel says then, and I'm thrown by my son's sudden show of support for his partner. How can he be in on this nonsense as well? Haven might be crazy, but I thought my son had more sense than this.

'How can it be true?' I cry, abandoning any urge to try and stay calm considering we are in a public place, and a well-educated woman is sitting on the other side of this desk watching this family fiasco unfolding before her eyes. 'You met my son in Australia and Valerie died here in England before you came back. You were on the other side of the world when my mother lost her life, so how can you stand there and spout this nonsense about having known her?'

'Just because you don't understand something, it doesn't mean it didn't happen,' Haven says plainly.

I swear in this moment I could reach out and slap her. I actually don't know how I resist, but some part of me holds myself to restraint, which is fortunate because I'm sure if I did strike my son's partner, then mine and his relationship would never be the same again.

'I'm sorry. Do we need to reschedule this meeting?' Jane asks, intercepting this curious conversation as professionally as she can.

'No, we do not!' I snap back, though my ire is directed firmly at Haven and not the polite solicitor who was ready to get proceedings underway before we were all rudely interrupted. 'We are ready to start the meeting, just as soon as Haven has left the room.'

'I want her here,' Joel repeats, much to my dismay. This situation doesn't need to get any harder by being made to feel like I have to choose between my son and what is right. But there's no doubt that the right thing here is that this meeting only involves close family members and, unless Joel and Haven have got married in the five minutes they seem to have known each other, she does not qualify as a close family member.

'You'll understand if you just let me explain,' Haven says, though I very much doubt that.

'Then why don't you explain it to us?' Scott says with a sigh, my eldest not looking at all angry like I am, just seemingly annoyed that he can't leave here and go back to working in his garage already.

'No problem!' Haven exclaims with a big smile, as if the past sixty seconds of stress didn't exist at all. 'But can I take a seat first? It feels weird to stand when we could all sit down.'

Haven doesn't wait for an invite then, instead dropping herself into a vacant chair as if she well and truly belongs in this important meeting now. But that's a fact that I would still very much dispute, unless she has an incredible story to tell me about how she did actually know my mother after all. And then the story begins...

'You are correct, Liane. I was in Australia and Valerie was here, so I never actually met her in person,' Haven begins.

I feel a sense of relief washing through me because it seems this silly woman has finally acknowledged the foolishness of what she has said.

'But just because we were never physically together, that doesn't mean I didn't know her.'

I'm wondering now if she is going to say something about how Joel told her lots of stories about his grandmother and, from that, she believes she somehow 'knew' Valerie after all. If so, that would be quite the stretch and still not qualify her by any metric to be present in this room.

'We exchanged messages online,' Haven says next. 'Quite a few messages, actually. That's the thing about the world these days. You don't have to have met somebody in person to have gotten to know them. Not when things like the internet exist.'

Again, I could slap Haven for spelling out something so simple that it seems like she is trying to make me feel stupid. Of course I know the internet exists. I just had no idea it was at all relevant to this discussion.

'Messages?' I repeat.

'Yes,' Joel answers for her. 'Haven and Grandma Val were in contact with each other.'

'But why?' I can only ask next.

'Because Grandma had seen our travel photos on social media,' Joel answers again.

'Grandma Val was on social media?' Scott asks before laughing. 'Really?'

'I was surprised too, but yeah. She said she wanted to keep up to date with my adventures,' Joel says.

I had no idea my mother was on social media either. She certainly hadn't mentioned it to me.

'But you said you didn't want me stalking you online while you were away,' I remind Joel. 'You blocked me and only sent me photos you wanted me to see. You said you wanted space.'

'Yes, I know. I had no idea Grandma was going to pop up on social media, but when she liked one of my photos and left a nice comment, I thought it was harmless to have her seeing my travel photos.'

I had tried my best not to be upset that Joel requested me and his father not snoop on his every move online while he was away, but only because I accepted his need for some adult privacy. But now I find out my mum was allowed to keep tabs on him and she didn't even tell me about it.

'Grandma sent me a message saying that Haven looked like a lovely young woman and she was very happy that I was happy,' Joel explains. 'I showed Haven the message and she was flattered, so she wanted to write her own message back. That's how it started.'

'That's right,' Haven interjects. 'I messaged her from my personal account, thanking her and saying that I was looking forward to meeting her one day and then she replied asking a few things about me and life in Australia. We exchanged several messages over a number of months after that, so despite what you think, Liane, I feel like I did know your mother. I feel like I knew her quite well, actually.'

I'm not sure what to say to any of this, and my shock is currently rendering me speechless. But I do know that I don't want to potentially embarrass myself further by being adamant about something only to have it proved wrong.

'I'm sorry to interrupt, but I have another meeting scheduled after this one,' Jane says, reminding everyone else in the room that she is only here to do a job, not listen to our family affairs.

'Of course, sorry,' Frederik says and looks to me. 'Can we get this started, or...?'

'No,' I reply firmly, looking back to Haven. 'Okay, so you might have been messaging my mother from Australia, but this meeting is much more personal than that. Please, can you understand and accept my request to just wait outside?'

I can't say fairer than that, can I?

'Either Haven stays or we both leave,' Joel answers for her, putting me in a very uncomfortable position.

'Let's just get this over with,' Scott tries then and he gestures towards Jane to begin.

Everyone is now seated except me, and I remain standing as Jane looks awkwardly at me before I concede and give her the nod to begin.

As the solicitor runs through her opening preamble, which is mostly just stating anything that she is legally required to say, I can't help but stare at Haven. It feels like my eyes are boring into the back of her head as she sits here with my family, Joel to the left of her, Scott to the right and my husband also there. He looks back at me and mouths the question 'do you want to sit down?' but I just shake my head and look back to Haven.

'As you may have already been aware, Valerie had a substantial estate. As well as her home, which recent property estimates value to be worth somewhere in the region of four hundred thousand pounds, there are her savings too. It is these savings that I will go through first.'

I should be paying more attention to what Jane is saying because it's very important, particularly the property estimate, though it does sound in line with similar homes in this area of the North. But I'm still far busier scorching Haven's head with my steely glare.

'To her daughter, Liane,' Jane says, briefly glancing up at me before looking back down at the important document in front of her. 'As well as the house, she leaves you one hundred and two thousand, four hundred and thirty-seven pounds.'

Wow. All that money and that big house. I see my husband raise his eyebrows and look back at me. It's more than he thought we would get. He presumed we'd get the house, but £100k too? But I remain stoic. I'm still more annoyed that Haven is in the room with us than excited about any potential windfall.

'To her two grandsons, Scott and Joel, she leaves you each seventy-five thousand pounds,' Jane says.

I notice Scott's mouth visibly hang open. Joel looks surprised too, and my two sons share an amazed look, as they should because it's a huge sum of money to be gifted from their dear, late grandmother. It's clear now that when she advised me to save for a rainy day, she really, really practised what she preached. But it's what happens in between my two sons that gets my attention next.

I see Haven look to Joel and smile before she reaches out and gives his hand a squeeze and, in this moment, a truly awful thought occurs to me.

Is this why Haven insisted on being in here? Is this why she is even in a relationship with my son? Is she with him to gain access to his inheritance?

If so, I hope she has written a will of her own.

That's because I'll kill her myself.

EIGHT

LIANE

I've managed to keep my increasingly murderous thoughts about my son's girlfriend at bay long enough for us all to leave the solicitor's office and make it to a nearby restaurant for a late lunch. Having heard how much he stood to inherit, Scott, unsurprisingly, decided to give himself the rest of the day off from fixing cars. Frederik was done with work, too, and texted his boss asking for the afternoon off after some 'developments in the family'. Development is certainly one way to describe how it feels for my husband and me to have inherited a vast amount of money almost overnight. As for Joel, as he is currently unemployed, he didn't have to worry about work today, and given his chunk of inheritance, he might not have to worry about it for a while.

The same could possibly be said for Haven and, judging by the big grin that is still on her face, I'd say she is certainly thinking about the fact that she has gone from being broke to now in a relationship with a guy who has a substantial windfall coming his way. That's the reason why I'm still watching Haven like a hawk as we take our seats in this restaurant and are handed our menus by a friendly waitress. I'm watching Haven because I'm still trying to figure out if the only reason she is here at all is because she knew Joel was coming into some money and once he has it, she is planning to spend it.

I don't want that to be the case.

I really don't want my son to get hurt.

'Order what you like, everyone. Lunch is on us,' Frederik says before glancing at me to check I'm okay with that.

I have no reason not to be. I can hardly dispute being a little generous with our money now we are going to have so much more of it very shortly.

'That sounds good to me,' Scott says with a satisfied sigh. 'I think I'll have the steak.'

'Me too,' says Joel.

'I might order the salmon,' Haven says. 'Are we getting starters too?'

That could be an innocent question, or a cheeky one considering someone else is picking up the tab, but I let it go, mainly because Frederik tells her that starters are very much on the menu today as well.

I should make a decision on what I want for lunch, but the truth is, I cannot concentrate on the list of dishes in front of me. Not when there is so much going on in my mind. Mum's death. Mum's money. The impact the inheritance will have on mine and my husband's lives. The practical conversations that need to be had. The changes that might come about from it. But even more pressing than all of that is the worry I have that somebody seated at this table stands to gain from my dear mother's death despite never really knowing her. Of course I don't count any social media messages between Haven and Valerie as really knowing each other, whatever Haven might insist.

Maybe it's just sheer luck on Haven's part that her boyfriend has just inherited £75,000 at a time when neither of them had any savings, any income or anywhere else other than my house to live.

Or maybe it was a calculated plot on Haven's part to get exactly what she wanted.

Could Joel have mentioned to her during their time in Australia that his grandmother had saved quite a lot of money and that one day, when she passed, he would stand to gain some of it? It's possible, and if so, Haven could have taken that private information and made a plan with it. Why bother worrying about what she would do with her life when her travelling days were over if all she had to do was keep herself attached to my son and wait for his inheritance to come in?

'Are we ready to order?' the waitress asks after returning to our table, and despite me not feeling ready at all, everyone else seated with me says yes.

As starters, mains of steaks and salmon, as well as champagne and cocktails are ordered, it's as if I can see my mother's hard-earned money flittering away before my very eyes. I know Mum would have wanted us to enjoy the money she worked hard over her lifetime to accumulate, and she won't begrudge any of us having a lavish meal like this one to toast to her and the wonderful woman that she was. But I'm sure she would begrudge somebody enjoying this money who perhaps does not deserve to. Somebody like Haven, who might have seemed all nice and polite in the messages she sent online, but who may very well be hiding a dark ulterior motive beneath that pretty face of hers.

'Liane?' Frederik says and I realise everyone is looking at me, including the waitress, who has her pen poised over her notepad to take down my order.

'Oh, erm, sorry,' I say, realising I need to figure out what I want to order and fast.

I glance quickly at the menu and see a Caesar Salad on there, so I just order that, along with a glass of sparkling water.

'Is that it? A salad?' Frederik cries, feigning mock dismay. 'You've got to get something bigger than that, surely.'

'I'm not very hungry,' I say before smiling politely at the waitress as I hand her back the menu.

As she scurries away to pass on our orders to the kitchen staff, the conversation at the table quickly resumes.

'So, what are you going to spend your money on, bro?' Joel asks Scott.

'I think I'll invest it in the garage,' Scott replies rather sensibly. 'I could expand. Maybe hire another mechanic. Take on more work. I think Grandma would have liked that.'

'I like the sound of that too,' I say with a smile, glad that my eldest seems to have sensible plans for the money. It could be worse. He could be planning to go to Vegas and blow it all on bad bets and pool parties like I'm sure some single guys in their twenties would.

'That's safe,' Joel says to his brother. 'Safe and boring.'

'Okay, so what are you going to do with your money?' Scott fires back.

'I'm not sure yet,' Joel replies.

'There's no need to rush. Take your time and think about it, the money's not going anywhere,' Frederik advises his youngest son. 'Although don't take too long either because we don't want you living with us forever.'

Frederik and Scott laugh as Joel rolls his eyes.

'Don't worry, I'm sure we won't be with you for too long now,' Haven suddenly speaks up. 'We can get ourselves an apartment, can't we, Joel? In the city, like we talked about.'

'Like you talked about?' I reply. 'So you discussed my mother's inheritance money before you even knew how much you were getting?'

'No, that's not what I mean. I was just saying that Joel and I have talked about living in the city, and we always liked the idea of an apartment in one of those complexes with a pool and a gym, so we might do that.'

'With my mother's money,' I add.

Haven doesn't say anything to that, but she doesn't need to because I've made my point very clear.

'Is there a problem here?' Joel asks me then, his question directed only at me, not at his girlfriend.

'A problem? Oh, I don't know. Maybe the fact that my mother's body has barely had time to go cold in the ground and your new girlfriend here is talking about using her money to buy a swanky apartment in the city so she can use the pool and gym facilities.'

'I didn't say anything about buying,' Haven corrects me. 'We would rent, wouldn't we, Joel? And I would only do it if Joel wanted to. It is his grandma's money, after all.'

'Yes, it is,' I say firmly.

'What's going on here?' Joel asks me again. 'If you have a problem with Haven then you need to tell us what it is.'

That question puts me on the spot and everyone around the table is quiet as they wait for my response. I realise that if I say the wrong thing here, it could result in my youngest son falling out with me, and I don't want that.

'There is no problem,' I lie.

'Your face says otherwise,' Haven replies.

'Excuse me?' I snap.

'You're looking at me like you hate me, so tell me what the problem is,' Haven demands.

She asked for it.

'I don't know, maybe the fact that you have suddenly come into a lot of money by being with my son and it seems very convenient for you considering you have no job or place to live without him.'

'What are you saying? That I'm only with him for this money?' Haven asks.

'Maybe I am,' I say, which feels like a very foolish thing to admit when I don't actually have any evidence, but it's too late because I've already gone and said it now.

'How dare you?' Haven cries, but how else could she respond to that?

'Forget about lunch,' Joel says, suddenly standing up. 'We're leaving.'

'Wait, what?' Frederik cries as Haven stands up too. 'We've ordered our food. Sit down, let's try and enjoy it.'

'How can we enjoy it when Mum clearly has a problem with me and Haven?' Joel says.

'I don't have a problem with you,' I reply to my son.

'So just me then?' Haven asks.

I don't answer that question quickly enough to prevent Joel shaking his head at me before he leads his girlfriend towards the door.

As Frederik calls after them and Scott looks around for that beer he ordered, I realise I have made a total mess of this. It's not as if I won't get the chance to see them again soon though. They live with us, for now at least, until they sort out whatever apartment they want to move into.

That means I will have the chance to rectify this issue with them.

Or make it worse...

NINE

LIANE

'We've put it off long enough,' Frederik says to me as we stare at the front door of our house from where we sit inside our car. 'Let's just go in and get this over with.'

'Easy for you to say,' I reply, still staring at the door. 'You're not the one who has to get it over with.'

'Just go inside and apologise and then we can move on.'

'Apologise! But why should I?'

'Because it's either that or this could get worse, and none of us want that, do we?'

'Of course not.'

'Then just go inside, say sorry to Joel and Haven, and that's it,' Frederik says, annoyingly casual about this.

'It's not as easy as that,' I tell him.

'It can be. Just explain how you have been under a lot of stress lately with your mother's death. You're grieving and you haven't been sleeping well. You've not been yourself and that's perfectly understandable because losing a parent is hard. I'm sure they will understand and I know that Haven will appreciate an apology.'

'You know that, do you? How can you? We barely even know that girl.'

'We know that she makes our son happy and that counts for a lot.'

Damn my husband and his way with words.

'Come on. Let's get this over with and then we can relax and have a nice evening together,' Frederik says, taking my hand. 'Maybe open a bottle of wine later. Watch a movie. Just forget about everything that's been going on lately and try and unwind for the rest of the day. How does that sound?'

'It sounds good,' I admit. 'Impossible, but good.'

Frederik gives me a kiss before getting out of the car and I have no other option but to follow him. But this all feels so wrong. How can it be that I feel so uncomfortable preparing to go inside my own house? I have lived here for decades. I raised two children here. I have slept and showered here countless times. I have a whole history here. Yet all it has taken is one woman's arrival in my home to completely disrupt things and make me feel like I am now the one who doesn't belong.

It's time to readdress the natural order of things around here.

After going inside, the only signs I see that Joel and Haven are already around are the dirty plates and empty cups by the sink. Having walked out of the restaurant before lunch was served, it makes sense that they came back here and raided the fridge, helping themselves to whatever food Frederik and I bought in the most recent grocery shop. I haven't asked my son for any money since he has been staying here, not just because I know he doesn't have any, but because I am happy to have him here and don't need to turn my child's presence into some kind of financial transaction. I know some parents want money from their adult offspring with regard to the extra spend on groceries or bills, but it hadn't even crossed my mind to ask. But if him and his girlfriend carry on like this, they will leave me with no choice. Not only are they costing us more money by being here, but they are causing us more stress too.

'They must be upstairs,' Frederik assesses after checking the other rooms but not finding anybody. 'They must be in his bedroom.'

'I'll wait until they come back out then,' I say.

'Why don't you go up and see them? Nip any awkwardness in the bud rather than let it linger.'

'Why should I?' I snap, and I feel like I've been doing a lot of snapping lately.

'Because you're older and wiser than they are,' Frederik says with a gentle expression on his face. 'Waiting for a couple of kids in their twenties to make the first move is like waiting for the summer to start in England. We'll be waiting a long time.'

My husband is right and not just about the British summer, or lack of it. If I don't go and see Joel and Haven, if I don't make the first move, they won't come and see me, meaning we'll be left to wait for some inevitable and extremely awkward meeting in the hallway at some random point over the next day or so. I don't want that, not when I should feel relaxed in my own home, so I better go and get this over with.

Climbing the staircase, my legs feel as heavy as if I was ascending Everest and not just the twelve steps it takes me to reach the upper floor of my house. I could use a base camp halfway up to gather my thoughts, but I dare not stop because my husband will only tell me to keep going.

When I reach Joel's bedroom door, I take a deep breath and twirl my hair before preparing to knock. This is the same bedroom door that I would witness my son scampering out of on Christmas morning, my little boy all excited to see if Santa had been and left presents. The same door beyond which were all his most beloved toys, from action figurines to stuffed bears. The same door behind which I would have to rouse him when it was time for school and he was going through his tormented teen phase, refusing to do anything for anyone. And the same door behind which he would play music or video games loudly, requiring either me or Frederik to have to politely request that he lower the volume as it was nearing midnight and the rest of us in the house would like some sleep. But this feels different. This feels like I don't belong here anymore. This feels like me and my son are becoming strangers in our own home.

I tell myself that everything will be fine and then knock. When I don't get a response, I knock again. But there's still no answer, so I could just give up and leave.

Or I could push the door ajar and look inside.

I decide to go with the latter option, mostly because I don't want to go back downstairs and let my husband know that I didn't accomplish anything by coming up here. As I open the door, I prepare to be admonished by my son, who never liked me just entering his room after he reached the age of thirteen and decided that privacy from his parents was more valuable than visits from them.

But he's not in here. Neither is Haven. The bed is empty, and while the duvet is creased and showing signs that a couple of people have been lying on it, they are not there right now. The TV is on though, playing on a low volume, telling me that they were here not so long ago. Why would they turn the television off when they could just waste more electricity?

I don't know where they could be. Have they gone out for a walk? Are they in the back garden?

I step over a few items of discarded clothing that lie on the carpet by the foot of the bed, some of which belong to her, unless my son has suddenly taken to wearing lacy underwear, which I very much doubt. When I reach the window that overlooks the back garden, I check to see if there is any sign of Joel or Haven out there, but there is none. They must have gone for a walk then.

Figuring I have tried as much as I can, I go to leave my son's bedroom. But on the way, I see the mobile phone screen light up on the bedside table. I shouldn't look, but it has my attention and I see that it is Haven's phone. I also see what the message she has just received says.

> *75k! You lucky bitch. I guess you don't need to worry about getting a job for a while now! Damn girl, send some cash my way, please! xx*

The message is from somebody called Clarys and I assume she is a friend of Haven's. But that's the least of my worries. What troubles me is that Haven has evidently already shared the news from the solicitor's meeting about my mother's estate, the one I didn't want her at in the first place.

How dare she do that. How dare she openly talk about Mum's money like she's just found a winning lottery ticket. How dare this friend of hers get all excited at the fact that Haven doesn't need to get a job now.

I pick up the phone and glare at the words on the screen, furious that Haven has most likely been bragging about the money that will soon be coming her way, via my son.

But picking up the phone was a mistake.

I realise that when Haven asks me what I am doing.

TEN

LIANE

'Well, are you going to answer me?' Haven asks me as I spin around and see her standing in the doorway, a towel wrapped around her, and her wet hair falling over her shoulders. She's obviously just got out of the shower, which explains where she was when I came up here looking for her and Joel. I still don't know where he is, but that's hardly the most pressing issue at the moment.

'Why are you looking at my phone?' Haven demands to know, staring at the device in my hand that doesn't belong to me.

'I wasn't looking at it. I was just...'

'Just what?'

I have no idea what to say. Of course I was looking at it.

'What's going on?' the voice behind Haven says, and I see Joel entering the bedroom. He has a towel around his waist and, like his girlfriend, his hair is also wet, and it doesn't take a genius to figure out where they have both been. So that's why I couldn't find them. They were in the bathroom together, taking a shower, making the most of having the house to themselves.

Except they don't have it to themselves anymore. But I really wish they did.

'Ask your mother,' Haven snaps, answering Joel's question. 'I just walked in here and found her looking at my phone.'

'What?' my son cries, looking towards me, and it doesn't help my case that I am still holding Haven's phone. I quickly put it back down on the bedside table but it's already far too late, so I better start talking, and fast.

'I came up here because I wanted to talk about what happened back at the restaurant,' I say, before realising I need to go a little further than that. 'I was going to apologise for any misunderstanding.'

'Misunderstanding?' Haven repeats. 'You accused me of being with your son for his inheritance.'

'Yeah, that was a really horrible thing to say, Mum,' Joel adds.

'I know it was and that's why I'm here to say sorry. I've just been under a lot of stress lately. Mum's death has hit me hard and I haven't been myself. You see that, don't you, Joel? You see that I've not been myself.'

Joel looks like he has to admit that and nods.

'It's fine, don't worry about it,' Haven says then, quite surprisingly. 'But I'd appreciate it if you didn't come in here and snoop around my personal belongings. You have no right to do that. I am entitled to privacy, even in your home.'

'I wasn't snooping!'

'It kind of looks like you were, Mum,' Joel says.

There is no way I can talk myself out of this, so I just concede defeat, for the sake of avoiding any more arguments or awkwardness. But I wish I could just remind Haven that she is in my house and I am entitled to do what I like here, in this place that I pay for, not her. Okay, so I shouldn't have looked at her phone. But she shouldn't have given me reason to go looking at it.

'I think I better go downstairs,' I say, heading for the door and, thankfully, both Joel and Haven step aside, allowing me to pass without any more questions.

In different circumstances, I might feel uneasy that the two of them had been sharing a shower in our bathroom while Frederik and I were out, but that's the last thing on my mind as I go back downstairs to find my husband. All I can think about is how it doesn't feel like I have made the situation any better. Then there's the message I saw on Haven's phone, which only strengthens my worry that Haven is hanging around this family for cash and nothing else.

* * *

I find Frederik sitting on the sofa, a glass of water in hand and an old war movie on the television. I wish I could switch off and relax as easily as he clearly can, but us women are wired very differently to men and I'm not the first person to notice that.

'How did it go?' he asks me casually, as if all I had been sent to do was complete a menial errand rather than navigate a complex conversation with a close family member and their difficult partner.

'I think I made things worse,' I admit as I slump down onto the sofa next to him.

'What? How did you do that?' Frederik cries, turning off the television to give me his full attention. He's looking at me as if it was impossible for me to make things worse, but that's only because he doesn't know what I am capable of yet.

'Haven caught me looking at her phone,' I confess.

Frederik's eyebrows go up, so I quickly speak before he can ask the obvious questions.

'I knocked on Joel's bedroom door, but there was no answer so I went in. They weren't in there so...'

'So you looked at Haven's phone instead of just leaving?' Frederik assumes.

'No, not quite. I mean, yes, I suppose that is what happened. But I wasn't planning to look at it. She got a message and it flashed up and got my attention, so I looked at it and I'm glad I did because—'

'Just stop,' Frederik says, cutting me off. 'Can we just agree that you should not have been looking at Haven's phone without permission, no matter what you might have seen on there? She's a guest in this house and she deserves to have her privacy.'

'You haven't let me tell you what I saw on there,' I cry.

'I don't care! It's none of our business!' Frederik fires back. 'And whatever you may have seen is not the point. The point is you shouldn't be going anywhere near her private property. How would you feel if she was looking at your phone?'

'This is different.'

'How?'

'Because I'm a mother and I'm trying to make sure my son is okay.'

'Of course he's okay. He has a girlfriend and he has just inherited a lot of money. I'd say he's doing fine.'

'That's the problem. It's the money! What if Haven is only with him because she knew his grandma was going to leave him a small fortune when she died?'

'I really hope you didn't go up there and accuse her of that again like you did at the restaurant,' Frederik says, shaking his head.

'No, I didn't,' I assure him. 'But I did see a message on her phone from a friend, and it was clear Haven has already been telling people about the money she has just got access to.'

'Did she see you looking at her phone?'

My silence gives Frederik his answer.

'Oh, Liane,' he sighs. 'That isn't good.'

'I know it isn't, but I apologised to her and Joel and told them I was under a lot of stress lately and I think they understood.'

'Let's hope they did, or things aren't going to get any easier around here, are they?' my husband says before getting up off the sofa.

'Where are you going?' I ask him before he can leave the room.

'I'm giving you some time to yourself.'

'I don't need to be by myself.'

'I think that you do,' Frederik says before departing, and the silence that follows is almost as uncomfortable as the conversation I had to have upstairs with Haven.

I get what my husband is trying to do. He wants me to take a break. Relax. Unwind. Hopefully emerge from this day a calmer, happier person. But it's going to take more than a few hours by myself to feel any better about things. My worries about Haven aren't just magically going to go away, nor are the consequences of Mum's death.

In all the craziness and confusion of today, I've barely had time to think about the vast sum of money that my mother has left to me and my husband. It's genuinely life-changing in so much that Frederik and I could take early retirement now and both of us could spend these next few years enjoying our fifties, rather than just surviving them as we eke our way closer to our pensions. I know it's what my mother would have wanted. Why else would she leave so much to me? But what she would not have wanted is to see that there were cracks forming in her family. She would not have liked the signs that a domestic war was on the horizon. She certainly would have hated the idea that me and my son could fall out to the point where we might not speak anymore.

I fear that might be what is going to happen.

There appear to be only three ways that it won't.

One, I come to realise Haven has genuinely good intentions and my worries are misplaced.

Two, Joel and Haven break up, and that seems unlikely considering how loved up they appear to be.

Or three, I decide to get rid of her myself.

As I sit here on my own and ponder all those possibilities, one of them seems more likely than the rest.

No prizes for guessing which one it is...

ELEVEN

LIANE

Another day begins with me coming downstairs to another mess. I already know it's a mess that has Haven's fingerprints all over it, not that I've hired any forensic experts to actually check the plates and glasses for those. I just know it was her because this is exactly like the mess that existed the other morning, so once again, she and Joel have come down here in the night and then gone back to bed leaving the place looking untidy.

At least I'm not alone this time. Frederik is still at home, and I better get used to that after the discussion we had last night in bed.

'Send your manager an email and tell him that you won't be coming back to work,' I had urged him as we lay on our pillows with the lights low. 'I've already done the same with mine.'

'That's a little hasty, don't you think?' Frederik had replied.

'No, it's not. You hate that job and now we have Mum's money, you don't need to do it anymore.'

'We don't have the money yet,' he had reminded me.

'But it's coming.'

'Yes, it is, but until it's in our bank account, we still need to keep paying our mortgage and our bills, so I still need to go to work,' Frederik had said rather sensibly.

But never one to be deterred easily, I had increased my efforts to show how much more fun his life could be if he stayed home with me rather than spend forty hours a week with his boss. It started by employing a few seduction techniques and rather than the two of us going to sleep at the same time we did every night, we tried something a little more fun. The kind of fun that we got up to a whole lot more in our younger days before real life quickly got in the way.

By the time we had finished, my husband's attitude had changed somewhat. Maybe it was the endorphins or maybe he had just relaxed a little more. Either way, he said what I was hoping to hear.

'Okay, I will quit my job,' he declared triumphantly, prompting me to give him a big kiss on the cheek. 'I'll phone in sick tomorrow so we can go over the finer details of it together and then I'll officially hand in my resignation next week. Hopefully the inheritance money will have been transferred to you by then too, so it's not quite as stressful. Then we've still got the money from the house sale to come after that.'

'Yes!' I had cried, although not too loudly as to risk waking up Joel or Haven in the bedroom down the hallway. That was assuming they were asleep and not doing the very thing that we had just been doing in here. Hopefully not, because no mother likes to think of their son like that, although the shower surprise earlier had left me in no uncertain terms about how intimate the young couple in my home liked to be.

'When do you think we will receive the money?' Frederik had asked me. 'Should it be by next week?'

'Jane said it shouldn't take long at all because my mother's will was very clear,' I had told him. 'The only thing we have to consider is inheritance tax, but there's not much we can do about that in this country.'

'A small price to pay for living the rest of our lives in freedom,' Frederik had decided, and I had to agree with him there, although it wouldn't be such a small price when the tax bill came. With that, we turned off the lights, and I snuggled into his shoulder until the pair of us had fallen asleep.

But now it's the morning and the warm glow of what occurred the previous evening has been well and truly replaced by the reality of a messy kitchen and the reminder that I am going to have to face Haven again very shortly.

Any hopes I might have had that her and my son would have enjoyed a long lie-in are dashed when I hear them coming down the stairs, and I prepare myself to put on a friendly face and welcome them into the kitchen for breakfast. But it quickly becomes clear that they aren't hanging around to eat. Even more so when they start to put their coats on.

'Morning,' Frederik says as cheerfully as he can, but I'm not sure if it's a genuine attempt at masking the awkwardness from yesterday or if he's just really chipper from his coffee and phoning in sick to work today.

'Morning, guys,' Joel says.

'Good morning,' Haven adds and now I'm the only one who hasn't spoken.

'Did you both sleep well?' I ask because that's the kind of thing a loving parent with nothing to worry about would say.

'Yeah, it was all right,' Joel replies. 'I think we're both finally over our jetlag.'

'That's good,' I say, noting that my son does look far less exhausted than he has done on previous days. As for Haven, she looks as immaculate as ever, her make-up already applied and her shiny hair smartly tucked into a ponytail. I guess she found the time to wash her hair in the shower, in amongst the other things she was getting up to in there.

'Do you want some breakfast or are you going somewhere?' I ask them both. 'I can make you something if you like.'

I notice Frederik give me a wry smile; it's not lost on my husband how hard I am trying right now. At least he is getting some amusement out of all this because I'm certainly not.

'Thanks, but we're going to go into town,' Joel tells me as he zips up his coat. It's the coat he didn't take to Australia because he didn't think he would need it and, based on the suntan he has come back with, I guess he was right.

'Oh, okay,' I reply. 'Any particular reason?'

'We're going shopping,' Haven tells me and then she flashes that smile again, the one that I'm sure quickly put my son under her spell, but it doesn't have quite the same effect on me.

'What are you shopping for?' I ask.

'I don't know, we're just going for a look around,' Joel replies. 'We can't buy much yet. Not until Grandma's money comes through.'

I'm almost relieved that it hasn't arrived yet because if it had, I'd fear Haven buying herself all sorts of fancy things with that money and I imagine Joel not possessing the strength to say no to her. Not if she kept showing him that smile. Certainly not if she keeps joining him in the shower.

'Would you like me to drive you into town?' Frederik offers, and Joel quickly accepts that invitation, so my husband goes to put his coat on too.

I decide this is not the time to broach the subject of the untidy kitchen again, and as the three of them go to leave the house, I realise I'll be all by myself in just a moment.

'Have fun,' I call after them, again trying my best to be friendly.

'I'm sure we will,' Haven replies cheerfully and, with that, they are gone.

I watch from the window as Frederik reverses his car off the driveway before it disappears down the street.

'Well, that could have gone worse, I suppose,' I say quietly to myself before leaving the window to get started on some of the chores I need to complete today.

I begrudgingly spend the first fifteen minutes tidying up the kitchen that I had previously tidied last night, before I go upstairs to clean the main bathroom. *I feel like this shower could do with a scrub*. Once that is done, I decide to do some washing, although there's not too many items of clothing that require a wash in mine and Frederik's basket. But as I pass Joel's bedroom, it's easy to imagine there is a rather big and growing pile of dirty clothing in there, as there has always been ever since he became a fixture in this house. I briefly question whether I should enter his bedroom after recent events, only to shake my head because it's foolish of me to even debate it.

This is my house and nowhere should be off limits to me.

Entering the bedroom, I see that the wash basket in here is as full as I imagined it to be, so I pick it up and carry it downstairs. Unloading the various clothing items from the basket and putting them into the washing machine, I check the pockets of Joel's jeans, aware that he often has a habit of leaving things in there that should not come into contact with water. Headphones, bank cards, important documents, things of my son's that have all been ruined by this washing machine in the past, so I am always careful to check now, just in case he's as forgetful as ever.

Miraculously, there is nothing valuable or important in my son's jeans, so I throw them in the machine. Then I come across another pair of jeans, and absent-mindedly check the pockets of these too. When I do, I feel a piece of paper inside and take it out, figuring I've just saved it from being ruined by the water when the machine turns on. But when I open it, I find it has come from the pocket of Haven's jeans, not Joel's.

I didn't realise she had put some of her clothing in this wash basket too, which meant I didn't know I was rummaging around in her belongings. But now I have the piece of paper, I can't help but read what is written on it.

Be careful and call me if you're ever in trouble again.

The strange message is followed by a mobile phone number.

As I re-read it all, I have so many questions.

What is she supposed to be careful about?

Who is this person she is supposed to call if she is in trouble?

What kind of trouble are they assuming Haven might get into?

And why does it say '*again*'?

TWELVE

LIANE

The sound of the front door opening makes me jump. Not because I wasn't expecting it, because I was. I knew it would open soon after Frederik left the house to go and collect Joel and Haven from town after their shopping trip. The reason I am startled is because I have spent all day troubled by the note I found in Haven's pocket and now they are home, it is time to ask her about it.

Or at least it should be.

But as my son and his girlfriend enter the kitchen, several shopping bags in tow, I chicken out of asking and instead keep the note firmly stashed away in my own pocket.

'Hey. How was town?' I ask the pair of shoppers as they drop their numerous bags to the floor and take a seat at the breakfast bar.

'Great, we bought a few things,' Joel replies.

'I can see that,' I say, eyeing up the bags.

'A few things? I'd say you cleared out a couple of shops back there,' Frederik says as he enters, tossing his car keys onto the table before heading to the fridge.

I watch as he takes out a bottle of beer before offering the youngsters one as well. They both accept, so he pops the lids off before furnishing them each with a cold beverage. He doesn't bother offering me one but only because he knows I'm not really a beer kind of gal. I bet he likes that Haven is. He once remarked, many years ago, that he finds a woman who drinks beer to be particularly attractive. I didn't think much of it at the time, but now as I stand here and watch my husband watching Haven take a thirsty glug from the bottle, that comment troubles me a lot more than it ever did before.

'What did you buy?' I ask, wondering how they could afford all of this when my mother's money hasn't been transferred yet.

'Just a few T-shirts to replace a few of the ones I lost while I was travelling,' Joel replies, and at least that sounds somewhat sensible.

'I bought a new dress,' Haven says next. 'I needed something to wear for when I meet all of Joel's school friends on our night out.'

I don't need to see the dress in question to know that Haven will look good in it, nor do I need to see my son's friends' faces when they all get their first look at their mate's new girlfriend. But I wouldn't mind getting a look at the receipt to see how much the dress cost. After all, I thought neither of these two had any money, at least not yet, anyway. Unless they're putting all of this on a credit card, confident they can pay off whatever debt they have accumulated when my mother's money comes through for them.

But considering the note I found in Haven's jeans earlier, it feels like I've already done enough rummaging around for one day, so I forget about trying to see the receipt and instead just think about what I have already seen. I haven't been able to stop thinking about the mysterious handwritten note that I discovered and I have been driving myself crazy trying to figure out who could have written it and what it could mean. I still have no clue, but despite that, I haven't shared my problem with my husband. I haven't told him what I found in Haven's jeans, mainly because I know he will admonish me for checking inside her pockets. It won't matter that I feel I had a perfectly good reason to do so, preparing the clothes for a wash cycle and all. He'll just say that I shouldn't be sticking my nose into other people's business and tell me to leave it at that. But there's no way I can leave it, not after I have read that note, so I will keep it to myself for the time being. Or at least for as long as it takes for Haven to realise that her jeans have been washed and the note is now missing.

It doesn't take as long as I thought.

'Are those my clothes on the radiator?' Haven asks when she spots one of her blouses drying where I hung it earlier.

'Yes, I did some washing,' I say. 'I thought I'd help out. I hope that's okay.'

'Thanks, Mum,' Joel says before swigging his beer without a care in the world. But Haven doesn't react in the same way, no doubt because she does have a care to give.

'Did you wash my jeans?' she asks me, her eyes scanning the room for any sign of that particular item of clothing drying somewhere.

'Erm, I might have done,' I say, feigning uncertainty because I don't want to make a big deal out of this. If I do, she might figure I saw the note, and I'd like to keep that a secret for as long as I can.

'Oh,' Haven says.

'Is that okay?' I ask, wondering if she might mention the note herself.

'It's just that I keep things in my pockets and I'm not sure if you would have checked them,' Haven says, eyeing me with suspicion.

'Don't worry, my wife is a pro at checking pockets before anything goes in the washing machine,' Frederik says, speaking up from his side of the breakfast bar where he is holding his beer. 'She has to be in this house because me and the boys were always leaving things in there that shouldn't come into contact with water.'

My husband and son laugh then, both reminiscing on all the times I gave them a lecture about not putting valuables into the wash basket with dirty clothes. But Frederik's rather correct assertion that I always check people's pockets is not really helpful to me in this moment, as I don't want Haven knowing that I checked hers.

'Oh, I'm sorry, but I didn't actually look inside any of your pockets,' I lie to Haven. 'I didn't think it was appropriate. Should I have done?'

'Erm...' Haven seems unsure what to say, so I speak for her.

'I'm so sorry if there was anything in your pockets. Was there?'

Will she admit it?

'There was something,' she tells me. 'A piece of paper. You didn't see it?'

'I'm afraid not,' I lie again. 'And I'm afraid if it went through the washing machine, it is most likely gone now.'

God bless the torrid insides of a washing machine and their propensity to destroy flimsy pieces of paper.

Haven looks disappointed by what I just said, as she might well be, given that I have just told her something she owned has now gone for good.

'Was it something important?' I ask her, leading her towards what I hope will be more information for me.

'Oh, no, it doesn't matter,' she says simply, but I can tell she is lying based on how quickly she puts the tip of the beer bottle in her mouth after speaking. Psychologists say that when people lie, they subconsciously try to stop themselves from saying more words, so they often put something in their mouth to cover it up as quickly as they can. While I might not have a degree in psychology, I have watched enough TV shows to know that

Haven was lying to me then when she said the piece of paper was no big deal.

She knows it's a big deal.

What she doesn't know is that I have it in my back pocket.

'Maybe in future, just leave my things and I'll wash them myself,' Haven says then.

'Okay, I can do that,' I reply as casually as I can.

'It's not that we're not grateful for you washing our clothes,' Joel quickly says, in case Haven's request came across as rude.

'Of course,' I say, swatting the air. 'Don't worry about it.'

With that, the conversation is over, and while I didn't learn any more details about what the note I found might be referring to, I did learn one thing.

Haven wants it to be kept a secret

Too bad for her that it is not.

THIRTEEN

LIANE

I'm not sure why I feel the need to re-read the note before I go to sleep, but I do, which is why I have it in my hands as I sit on the edge of the bed while my husband is in the bathroom. It's as if I'm scouring every letter written on this piece of paper for clues, not that they offer me any. I don't know who wrote it, nor do I know why Haven seemed too keen to not discuss this note further, despite thinking that I 'accidentally' destroyed it in the washing machine.

I'm just about to put the note away in the top drawer of my bedside table when...

'What have you got there?' Frederik asks me, and I jump because I hadn't realised he had re-entered the room.

'Huh? Oh, nothing,' I say, but it's too late because he's already seen the piece of paper and I assume he also saw how intently I was staring at it.

'It looks like something interesting, so what is it?' Frederik persists, and I don't think there's a way of me putting this note away now without it seeming even more mysterious. So I take a deep breath and then tell him.

'I found this in Haven's jeans when I was washing them,' I say as I hand it over to him.

'What?' he cries as he takes it.

'Keep your voice down,' I urge him, conscious of how close to our bedroom my son and his girlfriend are while in theirs.

'I thought you told her you didn't check her pockets,' Frederik reminds me.

'I only said that because I didn't want her to know that I'd found it,' I say.

'Found what?'

'Just read it.'

I wait as Frederik does as I say and reads the note before he looks back up at me with a furrowed brow.

'What is this?' he asks.

'I have no idea, but it's troubling, isn't it?'

'It's also none of our business,' Frederik says before turning away from me.

'Where are you going?'

'To give this back to Haven.'

'What? You can't do that!' I cry as I get off the bed and hurry to intercept my husband before he can reach the door.

'We have to give it back to her. It doesn't belong to us, and she thinks she lost it.'

'But then she'll know I was lying to her!'

I realise that I am now the one who needs to keep my voice down, but it's hard to do so when I'm panicking at my husband's stupidity. At least I have managed to position myself between him and the door though.

'Well, then maybe you shouldn't have lied to her, and you wouldn't have this problem,' Frederik says very unhelpfully.

'She lied to us too,' I point out.

'How so?'

'I asked her if the paper in her pocket had been anything important and she said it didn't matter.'

'That might be the case.'

'But it's clearly not because there's a phone number on there alongside a very mysterious message mentioning something about trouble. So I would say it is important, wouldn't you?'

'We don't know because it doesn't belong to us, so we shouldn't have seen it,' Frederik replies and he goes to reach the door again, but I move to block him once more.

'Just give it back to me. I never should have shown it to you,' I say, trying to grab the paper from my husband's hand.

'You never should have looked at it in the first place,' he tells me. 'Seriously, I thought you'd know better than this after what has already happened between you and Haven since she got here.'

'What do you mean by that?'

'I mean that you've already made some mistakes with your approach to her, so you can't afford many more.'

'Excuse me?' I snap, angry at my husband accusing me of making mistakes.

'You know what I mean,' he says. 'You've already accused Haven of only being with Joel for his inheritance money and then you got caught looking at her phone. I hardly think this is going to help things now, is it?'

'No, it won't, which is why you cannot give that note back to her,' I say. 'And before you accuse me of making mistakes, I'll remind you that I am only looking out for our son and making sure that Haven has his best interests at heart. I thought you knew that.'

'Yes, I do know that,' Frederik sighs.

'Then give me the note back,' I plead and, mercifully, he hands it over.

'What are you going to do with it?' he asks me as I go back to bed.

'I don't know,' I reply, but that is a lie because I do know.

I'm just not going to tell my husband because he's not proven to me that he can be useful when it comes to trying to find out if Haven is hiding anything. But my plan is clear in my mind.

I'm going to call the number on the note and see who answers the phone. Then I'm going to ask them about Haven and try to learn as much as I can about her. Based on what I find, I will know if she is still suitable to be with my son or not.

If she is, great.

If she isn't, I want her out of this house and away from my boy before she can spend a penny of his grandmother's money.

Most of all, I will want her gone before she can bring any trouble to my doorstep, and seeing as the note distinctly mentions the 'T' word, I'd say there is a good chance trouble is coming our way unless I can do something to stop it...

FOURTEEN

LIANE

I've spent all night thinking about phoning the number on the note, so much so that I didn't get anywhere near as much sleep as I had been hoping for. That might be my own fault, but it's not stopping me from feeling sorry for myself as I see the sunlight filtering round the edges of the curtains and realise a new day has dawned. But if only sleepiness was the worst of my worries. That would actually be a luxury.

Frederik has already left, going back to work after his impromptu 'sick day', though his days in that office are numbered now and he couldn't be happier about it. Neither could I. I have already given my notice of resignation to my employer and they know I won't be back, quickly replacing me with some other poor person who is as desperate for money as I once was. Now I have my freedom, but Frederik isn't quite there yet. He has to serve his notice period, but it is underway and I'm so glad he won't be leaving me for forty hours a week soon. Instead, we'll get to enjoy each other's company a lot more, like any married couple should. But for now, I have enough to occupy me.

Taking the note out of the bedside table where I safely

stored it overnight, I put it in my jeans pocket after getting dressed before going downstairs. Neither Joel nor Haven is out of bed yet, but there's no mess in the kitchen, so that's one positive. I decide to leave them both a note of my own and scribble down on a piece of paper what my plans are for the day so they know where I am if they wake up and wonder. Then I leave the house and begin the familiar walk to my late mother's property.

It only takes fifteen minutes to get from my home to hers, and I always liked how the two of us were close geographically, as well as close in so many other ways. One of us would often call around to visit the other and it's going to be weird knowing that Mum can't just make this same walk to my place that I am making to hers now.

My reason for going to her house is because it needs to be cleared out before it can be sold and I know it's going to be a big task, so I'm planning on getting started today. I can't say I'm looking forward to it, but I'd also be lying if I said it wasn't providing me with a welcome distraction as I continue trying to pluck up the courage to call the number on Haven's note.

I will do it today, I tell myself. *I just need a little more time to figure out what I will say.*

Reaching Mum's house, I take out the spare key I've always had for this place before taking a deep breath and slotting it into the lock. This will be the first time I have been back here since the day she died and I'm not looking forward to this experience at all.

As I push the door open, I hear several letters being dragged across the doormat, evidence of the post that has already accumulated here in the short time since the owner of the property has been gone. It's just a brief reminder of how life goes on and no matter how or when someone dies, the trusty postman still completes his rounds, totally oblivious to the fact that someone he is delivering to is now dead.

I pick up the mail before closing the door, feeling the cool air in here that is another sign of how uninhabited this place has been recently. If Mum had been here, she would have turned the heating on and kept it warm, but there is a distinct chill now and it's not helping me feel any more comfortable.

I pass the foot of the stairs as quickly as I can because I can't bear to look or linger at the spot where Mum died after she fell. Instead, I rush into the kitchen, where I put the post down before turning the heating on and then making myself a cup of tea. Mum always kept the cupboard well stocked with teabags. Once I have made my drink, I'm feeling a little bit better.

'Let's get started,' I say under my breath as I head upstairs to get a better idea of the task ahead of me.

I open the hatch to the attic and lower the wooden ladders before climbing up and poking my head through the hole. When I do, I see all sorts of things in the dusty darkness up here, from Christmas decorations to photo albums to dozens and dozens of boxes full of currently unknown items. All of this will need to be sorted through and eventually removed from this house before any new owners can move in, and I'm already regretting coming here alone rather than enlisting the help of a family member. Maybe I should save this for the weekend and come back with Frederik. Scott might help too. Maybe even Joel, if he's not busy with Haven. As it is, I'm on my own for now, so I locate a couple of empty boxes in the attic and take them down to start packing some items in the bedrooms.

I'm so engrossed in my work that I fail to hear the front door open downstairs. I hadn't locked it, but then I hadn't assumed anyone else was coming. That's until I hear my son's voice calling up the stairs.

'Mum? Are you in here?'

'Joel?' I say as I leave one of the spare bedrooms to look down the stairs at where my youngest child is standing. Unlike I just was, he's not alone. Haven is with him. *Obviously.*

'Hey, Liane,' she says with a smile, though it may not be the most genuine one I've ever seen.

'Hey,' I reply, a gesture that's not particularly heartfelt either.

'What are you doing here?' I ask Joel once that enthusiastic greeting is complete.

'We found your note saying you were here and thought we'd come around to see if you needed any help,' Joel says, and that sounds like a helpful thing to do. Or at least it would if it didn't involve Haven being in this house too.

'Oh, I see,' I reply, noticing how Haven's eyes are already looking around, seemingly inspecting this place that she has just wandered into.

'So, do you want some help?' Joel asks, and I can hardly say no considering the size of the task ahead of me if I try and complete it solo. Sure, I don't want Haven poking her nose around all of my mother's things, but I also don't want to be here forever trying to clear out the house, so beggars can't be choosers.

'That would be great, thank you,' I say. 'Maybe grab a bin bag from the kitchen and come up here. I'm putting a few things into boxes but there's a lot of rubbish that can be thrown away too.'

'Sure thing,' Joel replies, and he and Haven wander off to find the bin bags.

I return to my task and keep busy until Joel and Haven enter the bedroom that now looks marginally tidier than when I first entered it. While it's nice to have had a mother who was wealthy, a mother who made sure I was treated lots as a child, and a mother who I now have inherited a fortune from now I'm grown, it also means one thing.

My mum had a lot of stuff.

'Wow,' Joel says when he sees exactly how much there is in here, which is just one room in this sizeable house.

'Yeah,' I mumble back as I put several books into a box, none of which grab my interest to read so I'll be taking these to the local charity shop at some point.

'We'll get started in another room,' Joel says, possibly because it's practical to spread the effort, or possibly because he and Haven would still like their own space even if they have offered to help me out around here. But if it saves me having to make small talk with her then I'm all for it because that would be awkward considering I still have her precious note in my pocket.

'Be careful. Try not to break anything,' I call after them, offering a reminder that there are plenty of things here that hold both sentimental value and financial value and any carelessness could result in another form of loss.

I keep on working but can hear Joel and Haven chatting in the next room, even though I'm not actually trying to eavesdrop. It's just a very quiet house and unless one of us puts some music on, we're going to hear everything that we're doing. Not that I envision any of us doing anything particularly interesting here. At least I think that until I hear Haven say something to my son, something that she lowers her voice to say, although I still hear it, nonetheless.

'Do you think any of this stuff is worth anything?' she asks Joel, causing me to grit my teeth and stop what I am doing.

Is that why she's here? To check out whatever antiques my mother might have owned and to check if she can squeeze even more money out of the life that was recently lost?

I decide I've had enough of this and take out the note from my pocket. Without giving it another thought, I send a text message to the number.

Hey, it's me. Haven. This is my new number. Can we meet?

FIFTEEN

LIANE

My heart is racing as I wait for a response from the mystery number.

Will I get one? Will they reply quickly, believing that I really am Haven and agree to meet? Or will they sense something is wrong and ignore my request, figuring it's safer to do that than to take a chance on this being the kind of trap that it actually is?

I have no idea, but every second that passes is making me realise how desperate I am to find out what my son's girlfriend might be hiding.

I can still hear Haven's voice from the other bedroom, although thankfully, she is no longer talking about the potential value of any of my mother's belongings. Instead, she has moved on to discussing a TV show that she is obviously watching with Joel, the pair of them chatting about the latest plot twists that are clearly keeping them intrigued. I guess they're watching a lot of TV whilst holed up in Joel's bedroom back home, and I feel a brief glimmer of sadness for having all this doubt and paranoia about someone my son likes. But it's a glimmer that quickly disappears when I see I have got a text message back.

Is everything okay? Do you need help?

Yes! They replied! Whoever they are, they fell for my ruse and now I have a direct line of communication with this mystery person who is very close to Haven. So close that they are apparently willing to offer whatever help she might need, whenever she might need it. But while it's good news that they have replied, it now means I have the problem of figuring out what to say next.

As I'm pondering it, I get a fright when I hear a voice behind me.

'This book looks really interesting. I was wondering, would it be okay if I borrowed it to read?'

I spin around to see Haven standing in the doorway holding a paperback copy of what looks like some kind of detective novel.

'Yeah, sure. No problem,' I reply, just relieved that she hadn't got any closer to me because if she had, she might have seen what I was doing on my phone. She might have also seen the note I am still holding too, although I'm quick to hide it in the nearest cardboard box before she realises it is anything other than some rubbish I just found.

'Thanks,' Haven says before disappearing back to the other bedroom to rejoin Joel, armed with the book that she sought my permission to read.

I guess it was nice of her to ask if she could take the book, rather than just take it without checking with me. I have another sudden wave of remorse, as if I really should not be so mistrusting of her. But there's no denying that a note with the offer of help on it from an unknown number is unusual, so I want to investigate this as fully as I can, just to be sure. My worries about her motivation for money are one thing, but my worries for my son are another.

Looking back to my phone, I have a mini crisis of confidence as I worry that this is never going to work and I'm just going to make a fool of myself, or worse, cause a problem for my son that could force him to choose Haven over me. I don't want to do anything that could see me risk losing him, but I also don't want to do nothing and potentially risk something worse happening to him.

Eventually, after much deliberation, I make a decision on what to say next, which allows me to respond.

Can we meet at Harrison Park tomorrow? At midday?

I have no idea if I will get a positive response to that suggestion, but it's got to be worth a try. I've given an address to meet although I don't know if this person is in the local area and, therefore, if they have any idea where that particular park is. But I guess I'll find out. They'll either agree, say no or suggest an alternative location. But given how eager I am to get some answers, I'm willing to pretty much go anywhere.

I've just googled it. I can be there. What is this about?

The first part of that reply is good news. The second part puts me back under pressure. What shall I say to that?

I seriously consider my response before realising there is a way to keep this deceit going until the meet-up tomorrow.

I'll tell you when I see you.

I hope that will be enough. When I get back a simple *okay*, I know it is.

Putting my phone away, I can't believe I am actually doing this. I have a feeling I will be thinking exactly the same thing when I'm at the park tomorrow...

SIXTEEN

LIANE

It's a blustery day and the wind that is blowing through the park is only adding to the sense of unease I have about being here. But there's not much time for nerves now because it's almost midday and, as I look around, I see a solitary male walking towards me.

Is this the person I was messaging? There's nobody else around, so the odds are good. I study him as quickly as I can, seeking to gain as much information as possible from purely a surface level. It's not an ideal way to form an opinion of someone, not much different to browsing in a bookstore and basing your purchases on nothing more than a quick glance at the front and back cover. But sometimes that's the only way you have to judge it, and it's the only way I can judge this man before I potentially speak to him.

He is tall but not massively so, maybe just around six feet. His shoulders are narrow and his physique is far less imposing than that of my athletic eldest son. But what he lacks in physical presence, he potentially makes up for with a curious mind. I sense that about him by the way his eyes are darting around this park as he walks through it, and the hurried pace at which he moves suggests he is someone who likes to get things done faster rather than slower.

I watch him and his mop of dark hair get closer before he suddenly pauses.

When I see him stop, take out his phone and type a message, I wonder if I am about to receive something on my phone.

I do.

I'm here.

It's definitely him.

Okay, so I know the person who gave Haven that note was a man. A good-looking man, who looks to be a few years older than my son. Within seconds, my imagination is running wild. Is this her other boyfriend? Is this who she is cheating on my son with? Is this the person she plans to share my mother's wealth with once she has found a way to get as much of it as she can from Joel?

I can feel my anger bubbling up, but I must stay calm, at least until I have tried to speak to this person, so I start walking towards them. Because he's looking out for a woman who looks like Haven, he has no reason to pay me much attention as I get closer to him. But he does give me some attention when I stop in front of him and hold up my phone, showing him the same message he just sent me a few seconds ago.

The man frowns as he tries to figure out what has happened here, but I help him by spelling it out for him, deciding that I might as well admit to exactly who I am in the hope that it will lend itself to him being truthful too.

'I'm the mother of Haven's boyfriend,' I say clearly, though my mouth is so dry that I'm surprised by how confident my voice sounds. 'Who are you?'

'What?'

'You heard me. What is your relationship with Haven?'

Despite being afraid that this man might mean danger, I am forcing myself to stay strong or at least project some semblance of strength in his direction. More than anything, I'm trying not to think about how he could easily have a knife or some other sort of weapon that he might have brought here to use on me if he thinks I'm a threat.

'How did you get my number?' the man asks, his darting eyes scouring me for clues. 'That was a private number that only Haven should have had.'

'Then she should have been more careful with it,' I reply, hoping my false confidence isn't straying over into arrogant territory because that would be foolish. 'Now tell me who you are.'

As I wait for his answer, I remind myself that this is all for my son and his safety. Whatever Haven might have got herself involved in in the past, or at the present, should be her business and I'm only concerned because my boy could now be dragged into it.

'Where is Haven? Is she okay?' the man asks then, showing where his own concerns lie.

'She's fine, but I need to know who you are because I need to know if she is using my son,' I explain, again being as honest as I can because I want that honesty to be reciprocated. 'I'm just a parent who is worried about their child. Are you a parent?'

The man studies me for another second before shaking his head.

'But you might be one day, so you will understand how I feel right now,' I go on in hope. 'It's an awful feeling to worry about your child, but that's the curse of parenting. The worries never end. Fortunately, many of the worries are silly, everyday ones. But this one right here, this worry I have now, is a big one, so I need you to help me. Please can you do that? I'm begging you. Just tell me what you know about Haven.'

The man's eyes continue to examine me as if he is trying to determine if I am telling the truth. I hope he can see that I am. But what he does next suggests he doesn't trust me.

He looks like he's about to speak and say something important.

But then he just turns and runs.

SEVENTEEN

LIANE

I stand open-mouthed as I watch the man running away from me, unable to believe that he has chosen to run. But if I didn't think something very strange was going on with Haven, I sure do now, which is why I don't hesitate a second longer.

I start running too.

Going in pursuit of the mysterious man who clearly does not want to talk to me, I seriously doubt I'll be able to keep up with him, let alone catch him, considering he looks to be at least twenty years my junior. But I have to try because if I lose him now then I'll never get another chance to talk to him again. He'll never reply to any more messages I might send him, not now he knows I'm not really Haven, so I'll never have the opportunity to get any information on her if he gets away from me. So I keep running, as fast and as hard as I can, praying that I can reach him before he gets out of this park and disappears into whatever crowd there might be on the streets beyond. But it's not easy with stiff knees, and as I rapidly run out of breath, I am regretting even trying to chase this man down in the first place. But I can't give up. I can't just quit like I used to in all those PE classes back when I was a schoolgirl. This isn't just some silly test from a teacher. This is important adult stuff, so I have to keep going and tap into reserves I didn't even know I possessed.

'Hey! Come back!' I call after the fleeing man, but it's a waste of my diminishing oxygen levels because the man ignores me. He doesn't even turn back to check if I am chasing him, or how close I might be, which suggests he isn't too worried about being able to outpace me if he has to.

I'm already aware I'm not going to catch up to him without some stroke of fortune going my way, but as the man darts through one of the park exits, I'm prepared to give up on any such luck coming my way. That's until I hear the loud screeching of tyres. As I exit the park, I'm shocked to see the man lying on the ground in front of a car.

I see the driver of the car sat behind the wheel looking stunned, as if he did not expect to have somebody run right in front of his vehicle. For a second, I wonder if the injuries to the man I was pursuing might have been fatal. But then I see him trying to get back to his feet and I realise he isn't hurt badly at all, meaning he's likely to start running again any second now.

Seizing my chance, I reach him and stand over him, making it harder for him to get up. I'm not just doing it because I need to question him again, but because he might genuinely be hurt and I'd feel terrible if he got hurt because of me. But he does look okay and when the driver of the car calls out of the window, I realise this incident wasn't as bad as it could have been.

'What are you doing running into the road? I almost hit you!' the driver cries, telling me that the man lying by my feet was not impacted by the vehicle, so he must have just tripped in front of the car. That's a relief, and it means I can concentrate on getting this guy to talk rather than getting him to a hospital.

'Get away from me,' the man in the road says as he gets to his feet, looking a little unsteady, although maybe it's his pride that is hurt more than his body. I would be embarrassed too if I'd lost in a foot race with someone older than me.

'Are you okay? Do you need to sit down?' I ask, offering help. I would offer him some water if I had any on me, but I don't, so words are all I can give.

'Just get away from me,' the man says before grimacing, and I figure he injured some part of his lower body during his fall.

'Just tell me who you are, please,' I beg, trying not to be too forceful because this guy did just experience a potential near-death experience.

As the driver gets back behind the wheel to leave, I look to the man in front of me to talk. Thankfully, he does.

'My name is Calvin,' he says. 'I'm Haven's brother.'

'Her brother?' I repeat, processing this as something that I hadn't even considered to be an option.

'Yes, her brother,' Calvin replies. 'That's why I came here to meet her, but all I got was you instead.'

'But why didn't you just tell me that in the park? Why did you run?'

'I don't know, I guess I panicked.'

'Why would you panic?'

'Because I was worried for Haven and wanted to find another way to contact her to check she was okay.'

'I told you she was fine,' I repeat.

'Yes, but you also pretended to be my sister, so how can I trust you?'

He has a point there.

'I told you why I was doing it. I'm just trying to make sure my son is okay and isn't being used by your sister.'

'Haven would never use anybody.'

'You know that for sure?'

'Yes, I do.'

'Then why did you leave a note for her saying to contact

you if she was ever in trouble? What kind of trouble has she been in in the past?'

'It's none of your business,' Calvin says, and he tries to move past me.

'Yes, it is!' I repeat, blocking his way whilst hoping he doesn't try to push past me. 'I told you she is my son's girlfriend, and she is currently living in my house, so I have a right to know exactly what kind of woman she is and what she might be hiding.'

'She's not hiding anything.'

'Really? Because I feel like she is, just like I feel she is very, very interested in the money my son is inheriting from his grandmother's death. My mother's death. Money she worked hard to save over an entire lifetime. So forgive me if I seem nosey, but I will not stop until I know for sure that my mum's money is not going to be taken by somebody with an ulterior motive.'

Calvin has listened to everything I just said without trying to get past me or run again, which is helpful because I definitely don't have the energy to chase him one more time. Then he shows another sign that he is done with running, opting to walk over to the wall that surrounds the perimeter of the park we were in before taking a seat on the edge of it.

I walk over and sit down next to him before looking at Calvin to do the talking.

'My sister has been through a lot in her life,' he says. 'We both have. Our parents weren't there for us, so it's good to hear that you are trying to be there for your son. But Haven doesn't have anyone to look out for her, so that's why I will always be there for her if she ever needs me. But one thing I can assure you of is the fact that she is not trying to steal any money from your son or anybody else. She is a good person, and if she is with your son, then she likes him and he must make her happy. If so, it makes me happy too.'

That was not what I was expecting to hear.

'You say you have both been through a lot in your lives,' I ask. 'What kind of things? What happened with your parents?'

'It's personal.'

'I need to know. My son is involved now.'

'No, you don't,' Calvin replies. 'What you need to do is stop prying into Haven's life. What you've done today was ridiculous, and you have wasted our time.'

Calvin goes to get up off the wall then, but I put out a hand and I'm glad he stops.

'Just answer me this,' I say. 'If you and your sister are so close, why does she only have your number on a simple scrap of paper? Why aren't you two in more regular contact? Why have I never heard about you before? My husband asked Haven about her family and she just said it's complicated.'

'Complicated is the right word,' Calvin replies. 'And it applies to our relationship too. Just because I care for her, it doesn't mean we talk every day. She doesn't want to see me all the time because I remind her of the past. When she went to Australia, I didn't even know if I'd see her ever again. I thought she might stay over there and that I'd lost her forever. I wouldn't have blamed her because it's not as if either of us has anything here. That was until she got back and randomly turned up on my doorstep. She told me she had met a guy while travelling and was staying with him. She also told me she had a new number and wrote it down for me. So I wrote a note for her too and she took it before leaving. I haven't seen her since.'

'Wait, when did she visit you?' I ask. 'I was at the airport when she got back. She arrived with my son, and they have been staying with us ever since, so I don't know when she could have visited you.'

'I'm not making it up,' Calvin replies. 'She came to see me.'

'When, exactly?'

'Last Tuesday,' he says simply.

But that is not a simple answer for me. Not in any way whatsoever. That's because I greeted her and Joel at the airport on Sunday. So how could she have been in England before she got back from Australia?

'You must be mistaken,' I say. 'She didn't get back in the country until Sunday. It was just before my mother's funeral.'

'I know when I saw her,' Calvin reiterates. 'It was definitely Tuesday.'

'It can't have been!' I cry, but Calvin stands to leave, forcing me to stand too. 'Please, just wait. I'm only trying to understand all of this.'

'Haven doesn't need you snooping around behind her back,' Calvin tells me. 'I would get in touch with her, but I don't know which number to trust anymore.'

'Come with me to my house and you can speak to her there,' I suggest, but Calvin shakes his head.

'No, she wouldn't like that,' he says, and now he really is going.

'Please, wait,' I try one more time, but he walks away, and as he crosses the road, I decide not to try and chase him again considering what almost happened the last time I did.

As I watch him leave, there are still so many questions that remain. But I guess there is one main question that I need answering more than any other, so I call out to him across the street whilst he is still within earshot.

'Are you sure that she is not going to be trouble for my son and my family?'

Calvin stops and turns around, looking back at me across the road as a car drives in between us.

'I'm sure,' Calvin calls back before ominously adding, 'Unless you are trouble for her.'

EIGHTEEN

LIANE

I'm reeling from my meeting with Calvin for a number of reasons. One, I almost saw a guy get run over in a traffic accident – a guy I was chasing. I certainly did not want that man to come to any harm during our meeting and I'm glad that things didn't go any worse than they did. Fortunately, despite running in front of a car that almost hit him, he was okay. But I'm not. Not after being told that Haven came to visit him, days before I believed she arrived back in England. That piece of information drives a huge hole through her story and it's one that leaves me extremely puzzled.

I don't understand how Frederik and I could have greeted Haven and Joel at the airport after they'd flown home from Australia, yet she somehow visited her brother in England before that. I want to ask her how it's possible, but to do so would give away the fact that I tracked down her brother and spoke to him about her, and I don't want her to know. That's assuming Calvin hasn't already contacted Haven himself somehow and warned her about me now. Last but not least, I'm reeling because of the last thing Calvin said to me. About how

Haven won't be any trouble for me as long as I'm not any trouble for her.

That felt like a threat.

A warning.

A possible predictor of things to come.

I'm back home now after my ill-fated meeting with Calvin and I have even more questions than when I went to see him. That wasn't the point. By now, I was hoping I'd have had my worries eased and be free to enjoy watching my son and his blossoming relationship with his partner. Instead, I cannot stop thinking about how there is something very sinister going on that my son is caught up in, possibly unwittingly, and it is only going to get worse unless I can figure all this out before it does.

'Are you okay, Mum?'

Joel's question snaps me out of the trance that I have been in ever since I got back from the park. I had the house to myself for the first few hours after my return, but now I am very much surrounded by other people.

Joel's here, Frederik's here, and she is here.

'Yeah, I'm fine,' I reply, twirling my hair and smiling weakly.

We're all sitting on the sofas in the living room, watching something on TV. I say 'something' because I have no idea what it is that we're supposed to be watching. I haven't been paying any attention to it since my son selected it for us all to watch. I've just been sitting here, staring into space while my husband scoffs peanuts and the younger two snuggle up to each other on the other sofa.

I want to ask them both about when they actually got back from Australia. Find out if there's any way it is even remotely possible that Haven could have got back earlier and visited her brother before meeting me. But I haven't asked the question yet. I'm too scared to. Once I do, Haven will know I've been looking into her, and I'll have lost any element of surprise I once had.

Therefore, if she is hiding something, I'll be even less likely to find out what it is.

Her laughter cuts through the room then. She's amused at something that has just happened on screen. But the sound of it, juxtaposed with my personal paranoia, is jarring, and it feels like the lilt of her laughter penetrates my skull and makes a mockery of all my concerns. How can she sit there so contented when I'm so tormented? But it's what she does next that really makes my blood boil. She leans into Joel and whispers something in his ear. She probably assumes I'm too focused on the TV to hear what she is about to say, but she is wrong and I hear it perfectly.

'Let's ditch the oldies and go to bed.'

Okay, so she might not be the first youngster to refer to her boyfriend's parents as 'oldies', but given everything else that has happened lately, it's too much disrespect, even for me.

'You don't need to whisper in this house,' I say to Haven, surprising her with my sudden statement. 'If you have something to say to my son, you can say it louder.'

Haven looks surprised, as does Joel. Even Frederik pauses his peanut eating to look at me.

'I'm just saying, there are no secrets in this house,' I go on. 'None at all.'

Does she get that hint? Does she know that I am onto her? If she does, she doesn't give anything away, simply looking at me and nodding before stifling what appears to be a fake yawn in an attempt to get Joel to suggest they go to bed and leave us behind.

'I think we're going to go upstairs,' Joel says, and with that, the pair of them get off the sofa and head for the door.

'You're not watching the end of the movie?' Frederik asks before popping another peanut in his mouth.

'No, we're tired,' Joel replies before he and Haven leave.

'Guess it's just us two,' my husband says, smiling before

settling back to watch the rest of the movie. But I still can't give it any of my attention, especially not when I have an idea as to how to potentially find out more about Haven without her knowing. It's a dangerous idea, one that I'm not sure I can pull off, but now that I have it, I cannot stop thinking about it. It is very risky and it will be disastrous if I get caught, but if I succeed, I just might finally find out who Haven really is and what she is hiding.

So I'm going to do it.

Tonight.

'How long is left?' I ask my husband, referring to the film that I haven't watched any of so far.

'About fifteen minutes,' he says, and I think that's fine because I need to allow some more time to pass. I need Haven and Joel to do whatever they are going to do upstairs and then fall asleep. My plan will only work if they are not awake.

I impatiently sit through the rest of the movie, not at all getting any of the pleasure that Frederik seems to get from the huge twist at the end, but that's just the price I pay for not following the rest of the story before that. As the credits roll, Frederik lets out a satisfied sigh, possibly from the quality of the movie he just watched, or possibly from the quantity of peanuts he just consumed. Either way, he seems happy as he suggests we go upstairs to bed. But I'm happy too, at least as much as I can be, because as we head up, I am getting closer to being able to enact my dangerous plan, the one I concocted on the sofa when it would have appeared like I was not doing anything of the sort. As we pass Joel's bedroom, I can see a light on underneath the door, so I know they're still awake in there. That's fine, I will give it a while yet before I go anywhere near them.

I brush my teeth, change out of my clothes and then get into bed and Frederik and I make small talk in between him reading his book and me trying to hold onto the small kernel of courage I have about what I plan to do very soon. When the lights go out,

Frederik falls asleep fast, which only helps my plan. But I wait longer before getting out of bed because he's not the only one in this house who needs to be asleep for this to work.

* * *

I open our bedroom door and peer out and see that the light beneath my son's door is now off. How long should I leave it before going in there? Are they both already asleep? Or will one of them still be awake and see me creeping in?

I decide to wait a little longer.

But I can't put it off forever. If I'm going to do this, I need to be brave at some point and sneak into my son's bedroom to get what I want, so eventually, I leave my bedroom and creep towards his.

Reaching the door, I put my ear against it and listen in. I can hear soft snores. They sound like Joel's. I'd recognise that sound anywhere. But I can't hear her.

Either she's a silent sleeper.

Or she's still awake.

I swallow hard before reaching out for the handle. Then I open the door and go inside, hoping to get what I want.

But also scared of losing something precious at the same time...

NINETEEN

LIANE

As I enter my son's bedroom, I already know it's too late to turn back. If Haven is awake, she'll have heard me coming in and, any second now, the light will go on and I'll be caught standing here. But that doesn't happen. There is no light, nor are there any sounds other than my son's soft snoring. I wait a few seconds to make sure before taking a few more steps into the bedroom and as my eyes adjust to the lack of light in here, I can now just about make out the shapes of the two people in the bed.

My son is lying nearest to me, on his side because he's always been a side sleeper. She lies next to him. Haven is on her side too, her back to my son, her head facing out of the bed. Facing in the direction of where I need to go.

I take a very quiet but very deep breath before taking a tentative step towards the bed. I'm very aware that there could be numerous trip hazards on the floor by my feet, based on how many items of clothing I saw lying on the carpet in here the last time I came in. All I can do is be careful and hope that I don't fall victim to tripping over a T-shirt or getting my foot caught in some loose lingerie.

So far, so good. I make it to Haven's side of the bed, and my eyes are continuing to adjust to the dark room, helping my cause, like I'm some kind of nocturnal animal hunting for its prey in the dead of night. I keep moving until I reach the bedside table close to where Haven rests her head on her pillow, but before I make another move, I lean in to make sure she really is asleep.

I can just about see that her eyes are closed and her mouth is hanging open slightly, suggesting she is in a deep sleep, and she hasn't been disturbed yet. That's good, but I still haven't got what I came for so this will all have been for nothing until I have.

Looking away from Haven and down at the bedside table, I make out the dark shape of her mobile phone. I had assumed she would keep it on here while she was sleeping, as most people do as they charge their device overnight, and sure enough, here it is, plugged into the cable that goes into the wall.

All I need to do now is quietly unplug it.

I experience yet another nervous nanosecond as I pick up the phone and gently remove the charging cable from the bottom of it, careful to place the cable down quietly rather than allowing it to fall and potentially clatter off the side of the table. Now I have Haven's phone in my hand, but it's still no good to me unless I can unlock it.

The only way to do that is to get as close as I can to my son's sleeping girlfriend.

Leaning in towards her, I hold the phone towards her face and pray that there is just enough light in here for the facial recognition technology to do its thing. The only way for me to gain access to her phone's contents is if this phone thinks she is the one trying to access it. But will it work?

I hold the phone as close as I dare to in front of Haven's face and hold my breath. But it doesn't work. As I feared, it's too dark in here. What can I do now?

I look at the lamp sitting on the bedside table. Dare I turn it on, just for a second, so that there's enough light in here for this to work? It seems way too risky, but it's also the only way.

I decide to do it.

Through gritted teeth, I flick the switch and suddenly the room is flooded with far too much light for my liking. I quickly look at Haven and Joel, afraid that they might have just woken at the sudden brightness, and as Haven's body shifts, I hold my breath and prepare to get caught. But after an anxious few seconds, both people in the bed still seem asleep. So I don't waste another second. I hold Haven's phone back in front of her face and, thanks to the extra light in here, the facial recognition software does its job and the phone now unlocks.

I quickly turn the lamp back off and the darkness that ensues feels comforting. What is not comforting, though, is that my eyes now need to readjust to the change in lighting again, and I am forced to wait for several seconds longer than I'd like to before I can make my way out of the bedroom.

As I do, I make sure to keep tapping a few buttons on Haven's phone, to make sure it doesn't automatically lock again and force me into repeating what I have just done. But, after what feels like a very nerve-shredding few minutes, I finally make it back out of my son's bedroom and into the hallway. Once I close the door behind me, I can breathe a sigh of relief.

That's the first part of my plan complete.

But now to get started on the second part.

For this, I decide to go downstairs, well away from any of the other people in this house, even if they are all asleep.

* * *

I reach the kitchen and quickly take a seat before beginning my deep dive into Haven's phone. I considered sneaking off somewhere a little safer, like the bathroom where I could lock the door behind me, or maybe even the car outside where I could do the same. But shutting myself in the bathroom or leaving the house completely might make too much noise. All is quiet in the kitchen so this will do. Everyone's asleep. No need to risk disturbing them any more than I already have done.

If I'm supposed to feel bad for what I'm doing, I remember my meeting with Calvin and all the red flags I have already seen since that young woman came into my life. Just thinking about all of that eases any guilt enough for me to carry on with my plan.

I remember Haven mentioning that she was messaging my mother while in Australia, via social media, so I decide to click on that particular app first. I really, really want to read those messages and see what was actually being said.

I open the app and see Haven's profile photo of choice, one of her lying on a golden beach, presumably in Australia, her long hair falling down her back while her long legs lie splayed out on the sand. It's a dreamy photo, but it's a far cry from her current reality, in which she resides here in England, currently shacked up in a spare bedroom with her boyfriend's parents. There's no beach here, only me and my desire to make sure my son and his inheritance are safe.

I click around the app, looking for the messages section before finding it. When I do, I see the top message is from Joel. It looks like he has sent her some kind of meme, a joke that he must have thought would make his girlfriend laugh. It seems to have worked because I can see a couple of laughing face emojis underneath, sent to him in response by Haven to show her appreciation of the meme. But I'm not here to look at what messages these two have shared with each other. I'm here to see what Haven might have sent that Joel might not have seen.

The messages below are all from other women who look to be the same as Haven, judging by their profile photos, so I assume they are her friends, either in the UK or in Australia.

But then I see a message from somebody who doesn't have a profile photo. However, I recognise the name next to it.

Val.

It's Mum. This must be the account she set up so she could see what her grandson was doing in Australia. And as Haven said, my mother had been messaging her.

I open the message stream and see that the most recent message was sent when my mother was still alive. Mum has said that the recent travel photos look wonderful, particularly the images of the beach in Western Australia, and she comments on how she would love to visit there one day. She also mentioned that Joel's brother, Scott, is coming to see her later that day and she is looking forward to it.

I scroll up, reading the previous messages, wanting to get a complete sense of the scale of this chat history between these two people. Sure enough, Haven was telling the truth, at least about this. She and my mother did exchange several messages, and in them, Haven did say she was looking forward to meeting her one day. But then I see one particular message that causes me to grip the phone a little tighter.

It's from Haven to my mother and it's dated a couple of months ago. In it, Haven explains how her and Joel are running low on funds so they aren't doing anything particularly exciting for the upcoming weekend. Haven then says they are both looking for jobs to fund the next part of their travels, but unless they find anything, they are stuck. While I heard something similar from my own son because he certainly wasn't shy in phoning home and politely asking us to transfer some money whenever he needed it, I did not know Haven was discussing money with my mother. Just as I did not know what is clear from the next message, in which Mum says she is willing to send them a little money to help out. She also goes as far as to mention that she has been saving a lot of money for Joel's future, but if he needs it now, maybe it's best if she gives it to him earlier than planned.

This is it. This is proof that Haven did know Joel's grandmother had money and that there was an inheritance to be gained. Mum never told me she had made such an offer to Haven. She never mentioned that she was prepared to send them money in Australia. No wonder Haven was so smug when she told me she did know my mother after all. It's clear she knew her a lot better than I thought.

Before I can read any more of these messages, a new one flashes up on the screen. It's just been sent to Haven right now and, purely by accident because my fingers were already tapping the screen, I end up opening it.

When I do, I can't help but see what it says.

If you don't leave Joel and my family alone, I will hurt you.

What is this? Who has sent such a message to Haven? I don't know because the number it has come from hasn't been saved in Haven's phone, so it's just a string of digits I don't recognise. But considering what it says, it has to have come from someone in my family.

Who is warning Haven away from us? Who else has suspicions about her other than me? What the hell is going on here?

Before I can find out, the phone is suddenly pulled from my hand. When I spin around, I see why somebody snatched it away from me.

It's because it doesn't belong to me.

It belongs to the person who just took it.

It's Haven.

She's caught me.

Now what?

TWENTY

LIANE

'Give it back!' I cry as Haven checks her phone to see what I was looking at.

'It's my phone!' she snaps back and she's right there, so there's no way I can win this argument. But it doesn't matter that she has her phone in her hand now because I've already seen what was on it. I've seen the message she just received from somebody warning her to stay away from my family. I just don't know who sent it, but Haven is not leaving this kitchen until I find out.

'What are you up to?' I demand to know. 'What do you want here?'

'I can't believe you took my phone,' Haven replies. 'You're a psycho! Why are you stalking me?'

'I'm not stalking you, I'm just trying to make sure that my son is not making a big mistake by being with you.'

'The only mistake I can see is that his mother turned out to be crazy,' Haven snaps back, and if it wasn't for somebody entering the room behind Haven, I am pretty sure I would have slapped her for that comment. As it is, Frederik quickly enters, looking sleepy and confused, and he is quickly followed by Joel.

'What is going on?' my husband asks, presumably having been woken by the noise of the pair of us shouting down here. Joel too, and I see my son looks stunned at the sight of his mother and his girlfriend facing off in here like two aggressive animals in the wild, each looking for their next kill.

'Ask your mother!' Haven cries. 'I woke up and went to check my phone, but it wasn't where I left it next to the bed. I looked around for it but couldn't find it anywhere so I wondered if I had left it downstairs. But when I got down here, I found her with it!'

The way she says *her* with such spite hurts me, but it is most likely justified from her point of view. She does just see me as someone who crept into her room while she slept and stole one of her possessions. Now she has explained that to the men in the room, they are going to see me that way too. Unless I can talk my way out of this.

'Mum? Did you take her phone?' Joel asks, looking stunned.

'Yes, she did!' Haven cries, answering for me.

'Okay, I admit it. I took her phone,' I say. 'But I had a good reason to.'

'What possible reason could there be to steal my girlfriend's phone?' Joel cries.

'Because I think she is trouble,' I say.

'Not this again,' Frederik sighs, and I really could use my husband's support, but I'm going to have to work for it. But that's okay because I have the ace up my sleeve.

'Explain the message you just got,' I say to Haven. 'The one in which somebody just told you to stay away from this family. Who sent you that?'

'What is she talking about?' Joel asks.

'I don't know,' Haven replies, suddenly seeming sheepish and, for the first time, I see a chink in her armour.

'Show us the last message you just received,' I demand. 'I saw it flash up while I had your phone.'

'No,' Haven says, and even if she hasn't had time to look at it yet, she clearly knows the kind of thing I am referring to. Somebody is warning her away from us, and it's not me or Joel. I'm guessing it's not Frederik either, given how clueless he looks as he stands there watching all of this unfold.

'This is stupid. I can't stay here anymore,' Haven says, and she turns to leave.

'You're not getting away that easily,' I call after her. 'Or are you running now that you've been exposed for only being here for money?'

Haven stops then and while I have been successful in getting her to stay, the look on her face as she turns around tells me what is coming next is going to be explosive.

I'm not wrong.

'You think I'm the bad guy here?' Haven asks, looking at me as if I'm totally stupid. 'If that's the case then you really have no idea what is going on.'

Suddenly, the ominous lurch in my stomach makes me feel like I don't want to know. I thought I did, but now, judging by how Haven is glaring at me, I have a very bad feeling about this. But it's too late.

'Nobody is the bad guy here. Everyone just needs to calm down,' Frederik tries.

'I think it's too late for that,' Joel says. 'Mum, you need to apologise to Haven right now.'

'No, she doesn't,' Haven says, surprising me as well as everyone else. 'She just needs to listen to what I am about to say. You all do.'

Another ominous lurch.

What is on the tip of her tongue?

'I should have told you this sooner. I've let it get way too far,' Haven goes on.

'Told us what?' Frederik asks, and I'm glad he does because I seem to have momentarily lost my ability to speak. I guess that's what happens when you feel like you're on the verge of hearing something that is going to turn your world upside down.

'About what really happened when Valerie died,' Haven says.

There is a genuine pause then as me, Frederik and Joel all process that shocking statement.

'What do you mean?' Joel asks. 'Grandma fell down the stairs.'

'No, she didn't,' Haven says. 'She was pushed and I know who did it.'

None of us know what to say to that, but it doesn't matter because Haven carries on talking.

'It's the person who is warning me to stay away from you all. The person none of you should trust because he's the one who was after Valerie's money, not me.'

Haven pauses, but it doesn't seem like it's for dramatic effect. Rather, it's because she's afraid.

'It's Scott,' she says, stunning us all.

TWENTY-ONE

LIANE

A hush has fallen across the kitchen as Haven's last word hangs in the air.

Scott. My eldest son. That's who Haven has just accused of being the one who was after my mother's money the most. Not her. But then she would deny it was her, wouldn't she? How can she think Scott has done anything wrong?

'I don't understand,' Frederik says, no doubt speaking for the rest of the room. 'What are you talking about?'

'Scott has been trying to get me to leave Joel and leave this family ever since I met him,' Haven says before turning to her boyfriend. 'It's true. I know he's your brother and I'm sorry, but I'm not making any of this up. Scott is not the great guy you all think he is.'

'Enough,' I order. 'Stop this nonsense!'

'It's not nonsense,' Haven goes on. 'You said you saw the message I received when you had my phone a few moments ago. Scott has been warning me away from you all and it's because he has something to hide and I know what it is.'

'What is it?' Joel asks.

'I said stop!' I cry because I really cannot hear any more of this. But once again, Haven ignores me.

'I think Scott hurt your grandmother,' Haven tells Joel and, with that, the hush returns. Even I am rendered speechless, and for a moment, Haven looks like she believes she has got us all to understand what she just said. But it doesn't last long.

'Okay, I think this has gone far enough,' Frederik says. 'It's very late and I don't think anybody is going to say anything sensible at this time of night. How about we all go back to bed, and we can resume this discussion in the morning.'

'Didn't you hear what I said?' Haven replies. 'I think Scott might have killed Valerie.'

'That's my mother and my son you're talking about!' I cry, suddenly rushing towards Haven because if I can't get her to be quiet with my words, I'll have to find another way. Perhaps fortunately, Frederik steps in between us, and it's a good job that one of us hasn't lost their cool yet.

'Leave it,' my husband says to me, as if we're in the middle of a pub and he's trying to break up a fight between two drunken customers. But this is even worse than that unsavoury scenario. This is a domestic dispute, one that threatens to destroy my entire family, but how can I let what Haven just said go unchecked?

'I cannot have her in this house if she is going to be spouting a bunch of nonsensical lies!' I cry, pointing a finger in her direction. 'Either she goes tonight or I do!'

That rather dramatic ultimatum is not exactly the fairest thing I could have done to Joel, who now faces the awful dilemma of having to choose between his mother and his girlfriend. I should never have put him in a position like this, and I would never have dreamt of doing so under normal circumstances. But then again, I never expected to have someone come into my house and tell me that my eldest son had killed my mum for her inheritance money.

'Just let me explain,' Haven says. 'I know it sounds crazy but—'

'You're damn right it sounds crazy,' I shout back. 'Now get out or I'll drag you out!'

In my chaotic frame of mind, I've gone from threatening to leave to now deciding that Haven is going. At least that might take the pressure off Joel, who is standing beside Haven with a look of horror on his face. However he imagined Haven's introduction to his family going as he flew home from Australia, this can't have been it. And then I remember. Calvin told me that Haven had been to visit him before I thought she had got back to the country. If that was true, I need to know about it.

'When did you get back to England?' I ask both her and Joel.

'What?' my son replies.

'When did you land back here?'

'You know when we got back. You were at the airport to meet us,' Joel says.

'Are you sure you didn't come back earlier than that?' I have to know.

'What? No?' Joel says, and when I look at Haven, I can see she is trying to read me. I think she's trying to figure out why I am asking these questions. That tells me there is something here worth digging into.

'Are you lying to me?' I ask Joel. 'If you are, you are only making all of this worse for the both of you.'

Joel hesitates then, and now I sense I am getting somewhere.

'What is it?' I urge him to tell me. 'What are you keeping from me?'

Joel and Haven share a glance then, as if they are silently making the decision on whether or not to share a secret with me. Then my son speaks.

'I don't know how you found out, but yes, we came back to England a few days earlier than you thought we did.'

I can't believe it. Calvin was telling the truth.

'I don't understand,' Frederik says suddenly, and I'd almost forgotten he was with us given how quiet he has been over the last few moments. 'We saw you come out of the Arrivals gate at the airport. How could you have come back, yet arrive from there, if you were already in England?'

That is a very good question.

'Because we left England again for a few days,' Joel says, and as my husband and I frown, Joel quickly starts explaining.

'Look, I didn't think it was a big deal, and I didn't think you'd ever find out, but the truth is, I told you the wrong date that we were getting back from Australia.'

'Why would you do that?' I cry.

'Because Haven and I wanted a few days to ourselves before we came to meet you,' my son goes on. 'We knew it would be pretty hectic once we got here with Grandma's funeral and Haven meeting you all for the first time. She was nervous about that, and I was still upset after hearing about Grandma's death, so we both decided to give ourselves a few days before we actually got here.'

'What did you do?' Frederik asks, but I already know one of the things Haven did. She went to see her brother, though I wonder if she will tell us that or keep it quiet.

'I was really jetlagged when we got back so I slept for most of a day while Haven went to see her brother,' Joel says, and yep, that matches the story I got from Calvin. 'Then the two of us caught a flight to Amsterdam because we both wanted to go and do something fun, before we got here for all the heavy stuff.'

I can't believe this, but it's hardly the worst thing I've heard tonight.

'So that's why you came through Arrivals,' Frederik says.

'You had actually flown in from an international airport. Just not the one we thought you had.'

'Yeah, our flight landed at a similar time to one from Australia, so it was easy to make you think I was on that particular plane.'

'Wow,' Frederik says. 'You could have just told us. Why all the secrecy?'

'Because I felt bad if I came back and didn't come straight home,' Joel says. 'I thought you'd all be upset if I wasn't here to help with the funeral or Grandma's things or whatever. But the truth was, I just needed a little more time to deal with it all.'

'He was really upset when we got the news,' Haven adds then, putting an arm around Joel, and as I see how much she genuinely cares for him in this moment, I'm once again feeling bad for doubting her. But I still haven't forgotten the crazy thing she said earlier.

'What you said earlier about Scott,' I say. 'Why would you say something like that?'

'I can explain if you'll just all sit down and listen to me,' Haven pleads, and there's something in her eyes that makes me follow her request. She's calmer now, and she still has her arm around my son, which seems to be making him feel better.

Is she lying?

Or have I got her all wrong?

As Frederik and I take a seat, Haven and Joel do the same, and I watch as the young woman takes a very deep breath. Then she launches into one of the craziest stories I've ever heard.

TWENTY-TWO

HAVEN

It's time this family saw things from my point of view.

It's time they heard the truth.

'I really didn't want to have to do this,' I say as my boyfriend and his parents stare back at me. 'I hoped there was another way. I hoped I was wrong. But I don't think I am.'

I take a deep breath and begin.

'When I was messaging Valerie, she told me her grandson was coming to visit her,' I say. 'She was talking about Scott.'

'I know,' Liane says. 'I saw the message on her phone.'

Of course she did.

'Well, then you'll also know that Scott's visit was the day Valerie died.'

'And you think that means our son killed her?' Frederik says, looking at me like I'm deluded, which is weird because he has always been so welcoming to me since I got here. More than welcoming, in fact, and I think I know why. I'm not blind. I've caught his eyes lingering on me a second or two longer than they should sometimes. He's attracted to me. That's okay, he's just a man and I'm just a woman, though there has been no suggestion he will do anything to take things further. He loves his son and from what I can tell, he loves his wife too.

'What I'm saying is, Valerie told me Scott was going to her house,' I explain. 'Then she died. Coincidence?'

'She fell down the stairs,' Liane repeats because she said this earlier in the conversation. 'And I visited her that day too. I was the one who found her. Scott wasn't there.'

'But that doesn't mean he hadn't been,' I say. 'He could have left before you got there.'

'Why would he push her?' Joel asks me.

'I don't know, maybe because of the inheritance he knew he would get when she died. The same inheritance you told me about when we were on the plane home after we heard Valerie had died.'

I know Joel will recall the conversation we had at 38,000 feet in which he mentioned to me that his grandmother had told him several times over the years that, when she was gone, she would leave her family with a significant sum to help them all with whatever they chose to do in life.

'I didn't think much of it at the time,' I go on before Liane interrupts me.

'Really?' she scoffs. 'Your ears didn't prick up at the sound of an inheritance coming Joel's way, considering both of you had spent all your money travelling around Australia?'

'No, not at all,' I insist, and I'm telling the truth, not that Liane knows me well enough to know that. 'I just wanted to make sure Joel was okay because he was really upset about his grandmother. But I started to think about it a lot more when I heard what Scott said at the wake.'

Liane goes quiet again.

'When we got here, I was suspicious of Scott, having known he had been due to visit Valerie on the day she died,' I say. 'I got even more suspicious when I overheard him talking to someone at the wake about his mechanic business.'

'What about it?' Joel asks me, and if it feels weird to have my own boyfriend form part of this disbelieving audience, I remind myself it only makes sense that he would be unsure about this too, because this is his brother I am talking about.

'I heard him say that business hadn't been going great lately, but he had a feeling it was going to pick up soon,' I say, which is the truth. That's exactly what I heard Scott say to somebody who was asking him about his work at the wake.

'Life as a mechanic is always up and down, Scott knows that better than anyone,' Frederik says. 'What has that got to do with anything?'

'Because he was downplaying how bad things had really been,' I say then.

'How would you know that?' Liane asks.

'The same way you could have known if you had only looked,' I say, which might sound a little harsh, but it is true. 'You could have looked online at his business accounts. They are right there on Companies House, just like any other UK company that is legally required to publish their profits.'

Liane doesn't respond to that, presumably because she knows what I have just said is right and it's not my fault she never bothered to look. But why would she? Unless she had good reason to and maybe she never did. I didn't either until I was worried Scott might have something to hide. Like the famous saying goes, there's no smoke without fire, and just because no one else in this family noticed the signs that something was wrong in Scott's life, it doesn't mean that I didn't.

'After hearing what he said at the wake, and also having been aware he had been due to visit Valerie on the day she died, the possibility occurred to me that he might have really needed some money for his business,' I go on. 'And that was confirmed when I saw his latest set of accounts online and how he had an outstanding loan that was overdue, as well as the fact that he had very little in savings in his company account. He was still operating, but he was in debt and it couldn't last forever.'

'So from all that *detective work*, you think Scott killed his grandmother for her money,' Frederik says, and the way he used 'detective' tells me that he thinks I'm just some silly person who has watched one too many crime shows.

'I'm just saying that I thought it was possible,' I reply. 'You have to admit, it is rather convenient that he's struggling to keep his business going and he suddenly inherits a large amount of money after his healthy grandma "falls" down the stairs. In one moment, his money issues have gone away.'

I use my fingers to add emphasis to the word 'falls', to show I'm not quite believing that Valerie did take a tumble of her own accord.

'Scott wouldn't hurt anyone,' Joel says then, defending his big brother.

'That's what I had hoped,' I say sadly. 'Until he threatened me.'

'He did what?' Joel cries.

'Is this another lie?' Liane asks me, her eyes narrowed.

'I'm not lying!' I cry. 'I'm telling the truth.'

'No, you're telling us a story that we have no way to verify because the person you are talking about is not here to give their side of it,' Frederik says. 'So I think we need to call Scott and get him here so he can defend himself against this nonsense.'

'No, don't call him!' I cry, and in the process, gave away how wary I am of that man.

'Because you know he'll come here and destroy your fictitious story?' Liane asks me.

'No, because he'll come here and threaten me like he already has been doing. You saw the message he just sent me. It's not the first one he sent and he's done more than message. He has threatened me to my face too.'

'He's done what?' Joel cries. 'When?'

'After the wake, when he was here late and we had all been sat around drinking. Just before he got a taxi home, we were alone together. You were all in the kitchen and I asked him about his business. By this point, I had already checked online, so I knew he was in debt, but I wanted to see if he told me about it because I had a feeling he hadn't told any of you about his struggle. Am I right?'

The whole family cannot say that I'm wrong there.

'But as soon as I had asked him about it, he went on the defensive. Wanted to know why I was asking. I said I was just interested, but he seemed paranoid and told me it was none of my business. Then I asked him about the inheritance money and how I was sure it would come in useful. But he got very agitated. It could have just been because he had been drinking and it had been a stressful day with the funeral. Or it could have been because he had a guilty conscience and didn't like somebody poking around at the truth.'

'Nonsense,' Frederik decides. 'Scott would not hurt anybody, least of all his grandmother.'

'Unless he was desperate and drowning in debt,' I say. 'Otherwise, why get all defensive around me and tell me to stay away from this family? Because that's what he did and that's what he has continued to do. I don't know how he got my number, but he has it and he keeps telling me to leave, so he obviously knows I'm onto something.'

'Or he just doesn't trust you,' Liane says. 'And he wouldn't be the only one.'

'I told you I didn't want to have to do this,' I say, defending myself. 'But what am I supposed to do? Scott is the one threatening me and you're all treating me like I'm the villain here.'

'I'm not,' Joel says, putting his arm around me, but in this moment, it feels more like a token gesture than anything more meaningful. Now I feel incredibly alone in this house, even though I'm surrounded by people. But of course I'm alone, because all these people are bonded by family while I am the outsider.

I'm the outsider who has just accused one member of their family of murder.

'I think it would be best if you spent the night somewhere else,' Liane says then, and when I look at Frederik, he appears to agree with his wife.

'Fine, I'll go,' I say, conceding easily because I don't have the energy to fight this anymore. It already feels like I've been banging my head against a metaphorical brick wall trying to get them to take my concerns seriously, so better to quit while I'm behind rather than expend more energy on a lost cause.

'You can't leave,' Joel says. 'Where would you go?'

'I don't know,' I reply honestly, but I continue moving towards the door.

'Then I'm going with you,' Joel says before his mother objects.

'Think about this, son. Think about what she just said about your brother. Maybe it is best if she gives us all some space for a little while.'

Best for who? Me or them? But I don't ask. I just go upstairs to collect what few belongings I have.

* * *

It doesn't take me long to pack what little I have in this world into my backpack, and I guess I'm on the move again, just like my travelling times overseas. But unlike in Australia, I'm not moving on to another sunny shore for a spot of sightseeing. I'm stuck here, all alone.

I think about my brother and know he would help me, and even though Liane foolishly washed the note with his number on it, I had already saved it to my phone. So I could call him. But I've needed him to bail me out of too many situations in the past, and he deserves a night off. I'll figure this out myself. I just don't know how yet. At least I don't until I leave the bedroom with my bag and go back downstairs. When I do, I see something that could help me. So I take it without a moment's hesitation, and just after I have, Joel appears.

He looks upset. Like he doesn't know what to do. *Lost.* Just like me then, except he has a warm home to stay in with his family while I will be out there walking the cold streets by myself with no parents worrying about my wellbeing.

'Haven, please. Just stop and let's talk about this,' he says, but the time for talking is over for tonight.

'I'm sorry,' I say as I walk past him and straight out of the door.

As I suspected, it is cold out here.

But I keep walking.

Anything is better than going back to where I just came from.

TWENTY-THREE

LIANE

She's gone.

I should be breathing a sigh of relief now.

But this is far from over.

I only have to look at my youngest son to know that. I can see how upset he is about all of this, most of all that it has ended in Haven leaving the house. Where does that leave their relationship? I have no idea, but what I do know is that Joel needs me and his father at a time like this, so we try to rally around him.

'Can I get you anything?' I ask Joel.

'How about I make you a sandwich?' Frederik suggests. 'Or maybe you could use a beer. I know I could.'

Frederik goes to open the fridge and I'm hardly going to object if the two of them decide that they need a little liquid refreshment to help them process what has just happened. I might need some refreshment of my own too, because I doubt any of us are getting much sleep tonight. But before my husband can get a single drink out, Joel speaks up.

'How could you do that? How could you just throw her out on the street when she has nowhere to go?' he cries.

'It wasn't our intention, but she was the one who was saying awful things about your brother,' I say, defending myself and his father. 'You heard her. What were we supposed to do? Just stand here and take it all?'

'I don't know, but you shouldn't have told her to get out,' Joel is adamant. 'I need to go and look for her.'

He grabs his coat and heads for the door, but Frederik is quickly after him.

'Wait!' my husband calls. 'You can't just go wandering around out there in the dark!'

'Why not? That's what Haven is doing because of you two!' Joel hisses back, and I should have known he was not going to be our best friend after what just occurred. But I really don't feel we had a choice. I have a family to defend and that young woman was threatening to blow it apart with her vicious tales of Scott's debt and motivation to see his grandmother die before her time.

'I'm going to go and look for her and you're not stopping me,' Joel says.

'Fine, but at least let me come with you,' Frederik says, grabbing his own coat.

'What are you going to do when you find her?' I ask my husband. 'She's not welcome back here.'

'We just need to make sure she is all right,' Frederik says. 'I know she's said some awful things, but it is late and it's very cold out there. I don't really want something bad happening to her on my conscience. Do you?'

Of course I don't, so I don't put up any more resistance and, very quickly, Joel and Frederik have left the house, leaving me all alone to pick up the pieces of what just happened.

It all started after I snuck into my son's bedroom to take Haven's phone while she slept. If only she hadn't woken up then none of this might have happened. But she did and now so many things have been said that cannot be unsaid. Only time will tell what the repercussions are from all of that.

I know I won't be able to get any rest until Frederik and Joel return, so I won't even bother going upstairs to try. Instead, I pour myself a glass of white wine and take a seat at the breakfast bar, hoping my drink will take the edge off my exhausted emotions.

I consider calling Scott and talking to him about everything Haven told us tonight. I want him to know that his family is on his side, not hers, so he has nothing to worry about regarding her wild accusations. It hurts me to think that he has been dealing with Haven and her lies alone, trying to rid this family of her and her venomous tales, without being able to lean on his parents or younger brother for support. It's not fair that he's had to face accusations of hurting his grandmother at a time when he is mourning her loss, like we all are. How dare Haven come into our lives and add extra pressure and stress onto a time that is already full of it?

It's late, so I hope Scott is sleeping now. I also hope Haven is not found. I don't want anything bad to happen to her, but I don't really want to see her again either. I want Frederik and Joel to return here without her, without having found any trace of her on those cold, dark streets. With any luck, Haven will vanish completely, realising that she has burnt all her bridges with Joel and his loved ones, so it's worthless to even try rebuilding them. But something tells me it is not going to be that easy.

'Oh, Mum,' I say out loud to myself, feeling her loss greatly now because she was always the person I turned to whenever I didn't know what to do. She always had some words of wisdom for me, some advice that she had gained from experience, something helpful to impart that would help me navigate the obstacle that was in my way. But those days are obviously over now. Never again will I be able to sit down with my mother and set the world to rights over a cup of tea and a biscuit. I cannot rely on her comfort or companionship, and that's a sobering feeling. But it's one I will have to get used to.

In thinking about my late mother, I'm also reminded about my role as a mother to Scott and Joel. How I need to stay strong for them and offer my own words of wisdom should they seek such a thing from me in the coming days. My eldest will need support against Haven's lies, and as for my youngest, he'll need support in losing a woman he clearly loved. Because that's what has happened now. He is going to lose her. I can't see any way back for her, not here, not ever. Wherever she is and wherever she is going, one thing has to be certain.

She is going to leave my family alone.

She is going to let my late mother rest in peace.

Or she will pay.

TWENTY-FOUR

HAVEN

Entering the home of a woman who passed away recently feels strange, as if I'm walking in the footsteps of the deceased, moving around in a space where their soul left their body and departed this world.

If I believed in things like ghosts and ghouls, I probably wouldn't have come here, as I'd be terrified that I might encounter the spirit of Valerie in this cold, dark house, coming face to face with her spectre at the foot of the staircase where she lost her life. Such a spooky sight would have me running back out of this house and into the night, screaming for the help of a stranger, but fortunately, I don't believe in ghosts. That's why, after using the spare key I stole from Liane's house when I saw it lying on the side, I simply walk into this house without fearing an apparition from the afterlife.

I close the door behind me but decide not to turn on any of the lights in here. I have to assume Valerie's neighbours know about her passing, so they wouldn't be expecting to see this property looking inhabited at this time. I can't risk anyone sensing something might be wrong and calling the police, so I'll keep this house shrouded in darkness. I'm only planning on trying to get some sleep anyway, so that should help with that too.

As I go upstairs in search of a bed, I tell myself that I'm not being disrespectful to the late woman who lived here, but just doing what I need to survive. I have nowhere else to go and it would be very risky of me to sleep rough on the streets. It's risky for anyone to do such a thing, but for a young woman who could be preyed upon by any shady characters lurking around at this time of night, it could be downright life-threatening.

Having messaged Valerie and got to know her that way, I have no doubt she wouldn't want me to be sleeping on the streets tonight. She was a kind soul, and no matter what might have been said, she would have made sure everyone was safe until sunrise. Unlike her daughter, who doesn't seem to care about what happens to me at all.

The staircase creaks underfoot as I ascend it, but every little noise is amplified in this otherwise silent home. Can it even be called a home anymore? Or is it just an empty vessel, waiting to be sold, and it will only become a home again when somebody else takes ownership of it and fills it with the sound of conversation, laughter and a little music or television? Until then, this house is in a state of limbo.

Just like I am.

Having been here before when I came with Joel to help Liane pack some of Valerie's old items into boxes, I have a rough sense of direction, despite the darkness. I know that there is a single bed in what is a spare bedroom just ahead of me, so I push that particular door open and go inside. The moonlight filtering in through the thin curtains allows me to see the bed I plan to make mine for the night, whilst also adding an element of spookiness to this uncomfortably quiet house.

It's even chillier in this room than it was downstairs, but I should warm up once I'm underneath the duvet that covers the spare bed, so I drop my meagre bag of belongings to the floor and try to get warm. Snuggling under the duvet, I don't know if I will achieve sleep but know I should try because I won't get away with staying here for very long, so this might be the last time I get to rest in a comfortable bed for a while.

Before closing my eyes, I set an alarm on my phone for 6 a.m. I figure that is early enough for me to get up and get out of here before Liane or anyone else in her family might call around to resume the packing. I can't afford for anybody to catch me here and have no doubt that Liane would call the police if she knew that I had been trespassing, so I will be sure to be gone early, just in case.

With my alarm set, I place my phone down before closing my eyes and letting out a deep sigh. This might be an unusual sleeping situation, but it's far from the strangest place I have laid my head in an effort to get some rest. Having had a troubled upbringing in the foster care system, the concept of a safe and stable environment is a rarity to me, not a guarantee. The same goes for my brother. Both of us know what it is like to sleep on the streets, in shop doorways or in homeless shelters, with nothing but a blanket, a stolen sleeping bag, or just the clothes on our bodies to keep us warm from the elements. That sleeping situation was often preferable to wherever the foster system placed us.

Many backpackers who travel around Australia and other such places think they are slumming it by staying in cramped hostels and eight-bed dormitories, but they have no idea. That's why backpacking to me felt like a holiday, even when I was sharing sleeping quarters with several other people and being subjected to their snoring, alarms or all other manner of noises they made at various hours of the night.

But I never told Joel about this fact. I have never mentioned to him that I know what it is like to not have a home and to wake up each morning with no idea where I might be sleeping that night. Instead, I just listened and laughed as he moaned about the state of the showers in one of the hostels we stayed in in Sydney, pretending that I was just like him and everyone else there, in that I was used to five-star facilities back at my parents' house in the UK like they all were. If only Joel knew the truth. But I kept it from him because I guess I'm ashamed of it. I'm ashamed of my difficult upbringing and how me and my brother had to do whatever we could to survive for several years as teenagers, even through times when we would steal food from supermarket bins and sneak into some unsavoury places to try and get a couple of hours of sleep. What guy wants to hear that their girlfriend has done things like that? Better to pretend I'm just like every other girl Joel encountered in Australia. Just somebody who was normal, up for fun, and didn't come with a load of emotional baggage that not even a highly paid, highly qualified therapist could hope to figure out.

I have no doubt that if Joel did know about my unorthodox upbringing, he would think it has contributed to what is happening now. He would think that my experiences have made me paranoid and a little crazy, and that's why I am making all sorts of wild accusations about his brother killing his grandmother for her inheritance. His mother would certainly think that if she knew about my background.

She's clearly a very troubled young woman and while I hope she gets the help she needs, you're better off without her, I imagine she would tell her son in the process of 'helping him' move on from me.

Liane might be right in that I am trouble and that I probably do need help, but that's all she would be right about. Joel is not better off without me, because I loved him. I still do. That's why I hope we can figure things out one day. It seems unlikely now, even ill-advised, but who knows? But one thing is for sure. I'm not going anywhere. I'm not giving up on my relationship, nor am I giving up on getting the truth about what really happened to the woman who lived in this house I am now trespassing in.

I believe Scott killed his grandmother and I am going to prove it.

Nobody is going to stop me.

Not Liane. Not Frederik. Not Scott.

I'm going to show Joel that he should trust me, not his brother.

I'm going to show everyone what kind of monster is hiding in that family.

I'm going to let the world know what I already know.

Scott is dangerous.

I realised it the first time I met him...

TWENTY-FIVE

HAVEN

THE FUNERAL

Meeting somebody important for the first time is a big deal, so it's best if the conditions are as perfect as they can be for it. The meeting should take place in a simple, stress-free setting, so both people are free and able to be themselves and present their best version to the other. There are lots of good places for this meeting to potentially occur. In a pleasant home. In a café or restaurant. Or in a park, perhaps. One place nobody really wants to meet for the first time is at a funeral. That's not perfect. It's as far from it as can be.

But a funeral is where I am meeting my boyfriend's brother for the first time.

Having already met Joel's parents at the airport, one potentially awkward encounter is already over with. But I can't relax until I have met the other member of my partner's family and, so far, I have not been face to face with Scott yet. He was apparently too busy to call by the family home when Joel and I got back, simply texting his brother to say that he would see him here, at this church where everyone is wearing black and looking glum. Or almost everyone is wearing black. Shamefully, I am wearing dark blue, but it's only because I couldn't find anything black that was suitable to wear for this. I don't want to come across as disrespectful to the deceased and I hope my attire is not suggesting that I am. I push those worries from my mind and think about Joel's brother again.

Maybe it shouldn't matter to me too much where and when I meet Scott, only that I do meet him at some point and that the meeting goes well. But it's not as simple as that. Not when I am extremely nervous about meeting him.

Not when I have my suspicions about him.

Not when I am afraid that he might be the reason this funeral is happening today.

As my eyes scan the sea of mourners here, I am anxiously looking out for the sight of the tall man who I have a bad feeling about. The tall man I have looked at in so many photos on social media once I knew he was Joel's brother and especially once I feared he was someone I had to be wary of. Even though I haven't met him yet, I will recognise him easily due to all the research I've done into him online, the hours I've spent scouring his social media pages to see if there are any clues that could confirm or erase the terrifying thoughts I am having about him.

The thoughts that he is capable of murder.

So far, I haven't seen anything extra to confirm them.

But I haven't seen anything to erase them either.

I've been worrying about Scott ever since Valerie sent me a message to say that her eldest grandson was due to visit her. That didn't seem troublesome in itself, but what happened next did. Joel got a call from his father, and when I saw my boyfriend's face fall, I knew it was bad news. *It was.* Joel's grandmother was dead, found at the bottom of her staircase after suffering a fall. She had succumbed to her injuries. She was gone.

In the initial aftermath of that nauseating newsflash from

the UK, all I could think about was consoling Joel. But as the hours went by and we began making our plans to fly back to England, I found myself re-reading Valerie's message. Maybe it was slightly morbid of me, but I found it surreal that I had only recently been in contact with someone who had since passed away. It was while I was reading those messages that I was reminded of Scott's visit to see Valerie on the day she died.

Coincidence? Harmless? Insignificant?

Or everything?

I've always been one to trust my gut instinct, a part of me that was honed during an unsettled childhood where I realised I could trust myself far more than I could trust other people. Barring my brother, nothing has steered me straighter in life than trusting my instincts, which was why I couldn't shake the horrible thought that Scott might have had something to do with his grandmother's death. If it felt crazy to think a person was capable of murder without even meeting them, I was hoping that finally meeting Scott today at this funeral would dispel those fears and make me realise how silly they had been. And then I see him approaching me outside this church with his hand outstretched towards me.

Now it's time.

'You must be Haven. It's a pleasure to finally meet you,' Scott says as he shakes my hand and smiles. 'I would say I've heard lots about you, but my brother is hardly the chattiest person when it comes to his love life.'

'Nice to meet you too,' I say, shaking Scott's hand and wondering if a simple handshake can indicate if the person giving it is capable of murder. As far as the handshake itself goes, it is a firm one, and Scott looks big and strong enough to hurt someone if he wanted to. Especially a woman in her seventies who would have no reason not to trust him until it was far too late.

Scott is wearing a smart black suit, and the smile he showed when he met me has been replaced by an expression that is a reminder of the sombre occasion we find ourselves at. I can't expect this man to be all smiles, not at his grandmother's funeral, but I also can't expect my concerns to just go away either.

'You both look so well,' Scott says to me, and to Joel, who has rejoined me after momentarily stepping away to thank a couple of his grandmother's friends for attending today. 'Must be all that Aussie sun, hey? Maybe I'll have to get myself out there one day.'

'But who will fix all the cars here if you do that?' Joel replies, a slightly sarcastic response that shows sibling affection between these two.

'That's true,' Scott says. 'It's not easy being the best mechanic in town, but somebody has to do it.'

I'd already heard that Scott was a mechanic – Joel told me back in Australia when we were discussing family, or rather, my lack of it. By the sounds of it, Scott has made a big success of himself, running his own business and getting to spend all day doing something he has a passion for. Thinking that makes me wonder what possible motive he could have had for hurting his grandmother. There's the inheritance that Joel mentioned to me when we were flying home the other day, but does Scott even need that if he is doing well already?

Then again, nobody would turn down free money, would they?

Frederik, the friendly father of the two men I am standing with, appears then to tell his sons that it is time to get ready for their pallbearing duties. I make sure to give Joel a big hug then, because I know how much he has been dreading this part of the day, before I go inside the church to find a seat amongst the mourners who have already gathered on the pews.

I do my best to push away any negative thoughts about Scott and the way Valerie died for as long as I can during the service, a service that is simple and sweet, just like that woman's messages were to me. There is a moment where I find myself making eye contact with Liane and I smile nervously at her, feeling awkward as I do because maybe a smile is the wrong thing in this situation.

I look away quickly and then make sure to study Scott as he carries the coffin into the church, watching him for any sign of something wrong. But he just looks stoic, so if he is hiding anything, he is doing a good job of keeping it covered up. Unlike Joel. Bless him, my boyfriend has tears running down his cheeks as he walks behind his father and brother, the coffin resting on their shoulders as we all watch on with sadness.

By the time we move on to the wake, and after consoling Joel with a warm hug, I am still watching Scott to try and get a sense of the man and his possible motivations. But it's not easy because if someone was a killer, they're hardly going to make it obvious, are they? But then I hear something interesting.

Scott is having a conversation with some guy at the wake and I'm lingering nearby, pretending to be busy sipping my drink. But I'm actually eavesdropping and I'm glad that I do, although maybe glad is not the right word for the sudden increase in tension that my body experiences.

'How's work going, Scott?' the guy asks.

'It's been up and down,' Scott replies, which doesn't sound like something the self-proclaimed best mechanic in town would say.

'Always is in that type of business,' the other guy replies. 'But I'm sure you'll be fine. People will always have cars, so they'll always need fixing.'

'Yeah, but costs are always rising and bills are getting bigger,' Scott says ruefully.

I know then that his business isn't doing well. He needs more money. *The inheritance.*

I try to stay calm, but it's not easy with so many scary

thoughts running through my head. But things get even trickier for me when I realise Scott has stopped talking to that other person and has now approached me.

'So, Haven. What are your plans next?' he asks me.

'I'm sorry?'

'Are you going travelling again?'

'Oh, erm. I'm not sure. Me and Joel are discussing it.'

'That makes sense. I guess you have plenty more options now than you did this time last week.'

'What do you mean?'

'Oh, you must know,' Scott says, clearly trying to read me.

'Know what?'

'My brother hasn't told you about the money he'll be inheriting now?'

I don't know what to say to that, but the fact that I have been asked it is a sure sign that the inheritance is very much on Scott's mind, as I already feared it was.

'Erm,' is the best response I can give to what feels like a very inappropriate conversation topic at a funeral, before I think of something better to talk about.

'Were you and your grandmother close?' I ask Scott.

'Close?' Scott repeats before scoffing. 'Of course, she was my grandma.'

'I know, but not everybody is close with their relatives, are they? I just wondered how often you saw her.'

'All the time,' Scott says casually before reaching past me to pick up a tuna and cucumber sandwich from the buffet table.

'Really? All the time?' I say, my instincts telling me I should perhaps shut up now.

'Yeah. Why? You seem surprised.'

'Oh, no, it's just that…' *Leave it, Haven. Don't show your cards too soon.* 'Well, I was messaging Valerie while I was in Australia and she said you were visiting her last week. I think it was on the day she died.'

Too late.

Scott's demeanour suddenly changes and he no longer looks like a guy trying to become friendly with his brother's new girlfriend. Instead, he leans forward and looks a lot more aggressive.

'What are you getting at?' he asks me.

'Nothing,' I say, stepping back slightly and bumping into the buffet table behind me.

'It doesn't feel like nothing,' Scott goes on. 'So why don't you say what's on your mind?'

I don't want to do that, so I choose to say nothing.

'Fine, I'll say what's on my mind instead,' Scott goes on. 'I don't know you, but I'm being nice to you because I care about my brother. But we're a close family and we look out for each other, so if you're going to be trouble, you're better off leaving us alone sooner rather than later.'

'Excuse me?'

'You heard me,' Scott says. 'Now, if I say I was close to my grandmother, then you better believe it and that's all there is to it. If you don't, well, let's just say my brother will be introducing us all to his next girlfriend sooner rather than later.'

With that, Scott walks away from me, leaving me stunned and silent.

Most of all, he leaves me feeling even more sure that he is capable of violence.

TWENTY-SIX

HAVEN

PRESENT

As I expected, it's been impossible to sleep. Maybe if I wasn't intruding in someone else's home then I'd be able to rest easier. Or maybe if I wasn't afraid that my boyfriend's brother is a murderous man who might hurt me next, that might help too.

After an hour of trying to get comfortable on this bed, I give up on sleep momentarily and check my phone. When I do, I see that I have a couple of missed calls and messages from Joel.

Where are you?

I've been looking for you.

I just want to know you're okay.

I love you.

I feel a wave of guilt wash over me, ashamed of myself for allowing Joel to spend so much time worrying about me since I left his parents' house and disappeared into the night. I feel so bad that he's been out there looking for me, although I am glad that he hasn't found me here, at his grandmother's house.

I need to message him back. At least let him know that I am safe. I don't even know if we can still be a couple anymore, but I do know that I need to be a decent human being and stop him from worrying all night.

I'm okay. I'm safe.

I think about leaving it there, but I can't.

I love you too.

I put my phone down and close my eyes again, but I can't help but wish that Joel was here beside me in the bed. Maybe not this bed specifically, because that would be a bit weird. But in a bed like one we have shared so many times before. Just the two of us, far away from here. Away from all this drama and stress. Back where things used to be easy for us both. Back before his grandmother died and there was suddenly a whole lot of money up for grabs.

I keep my eyes shut as if doing so will force my brain into sleep, but my eyes quickly open when I hear a noise downstairs.

What was that?

I sit upright in bed and listen out for it again. Then I hear it.

It sounds like something truly frightening.

It sounds like a key in a lock.

I get out of bed as quickly as I can and gather up the few belongings I had removed from the bag I'd packed. If somebody is coming in here then this place needs to look like nobody else is inside. But is somebody coming in?

When I hear the front door open and close downstairs, I get my answer.

Somebody is here.

But who?

I can't believe it. I thought this would be the perfect place to spend the night. I thought I had time. I didn't think anyone else would even think to come here in the middle of the night.

But I'm no longer alone.

Having picked up my bag, I creep as quietly as I can to the bedroom door, wondering if I can get a look down the stairs at who has just entered this house. If I can, I'll know whether I really need to hide or not. Maybe I'll be lucky and it's Joel coming here to get away from his parents. If it is, I could show myself and explain to him what I am doing here. He'd be shocked to see me, and shocked to learn that I stole a key to get inside, but it wouldn't be a total disaster if he found me because I know he won't want me getting in any trouble. But if it's not him, I will have no choice but to hide.

Leaving the bedroom and taking a risk to reach the stairs, I look down to try and make out who is here. But it's dark and whoever has entered has not turned the lights on. That's making it difficult to see. But then I make out the shape of somebody hanging their coat on a hook, and the slight glimmer of moonlight that falls across their face as they do it gives me my answer.

It's not a good one.

It's an answer that confirms I need to get away from the stairs as quickly and as quietly as I can so I can go and find a good hiding place.

I have no choice now.

I have to avoid the person who is here.

It's Liane.

TWENTY-SEVEN

LIANE

I hadn't planned to come to my mother's house tonight. I doubt anybody plans to go somewhere in the middle of the night. I should be in bed, my own bed, not here, in this cold house that reminds me of death. Yet here I am, and I'm here because I'm trying to be a good mother. At least that's what I told myself just before I volunteered to leave my house and spend the evening here instead.

Joel and Frederik were out for an hour before they both returned, neither of them looking particularly happy. That was because, despite searching, they hadn't located Haven on the streets and, as such, my son was still very worried about her.

'She'll be fine. She seems like a very resourceful young woman,' I had said to my son before quickly realising there was very little I could say that would appease him.

'This is all your fault,' he had told me as he stormed past me in the hallway. 'If anything happens to her, I'll blame you.'

I'd gone to respond to that but Frederik had silently and strongly gestured for me to resist, so I stayed quiet and gave Joel a few more moments to cool off. But it didn't work, and I discovered that when he spoke to me again.

'I can't sleep in the same house as you,' he said to me. 'Not after what has happened tonight. I need space. So I'm leaving too.'

'What? Where will you go?' I'd cried.

'I don't know. Maybe Scott's.'

'It's the middle of the night. Your brother will be asleep.'

'Then I'll ask a friend.'

'They'll be asleep too.'

'Then I'll wake them up!' Joel had cried, and I could see the pain all over his face. He was really cut up over what had transpired with Haven and how there was surely no way back for them now, and that was understandable. But what was not understandable was him going out into the dark night by himself too. Yet that's clearly what he was going to do as he went upstairs to 'pack a few things'. There was no way I could stand by and watch that happen, so I made a decision.

'I'll go and sleep at Mum's,' I said. 'Joel can stay here and you can keep an eye on him.'

'I think that might be the best idea,' Frederik had conceded, or maybe it had simply been far too late for another argument at that time. Either way, I went to pack my own things while my husband went to tell our son that I would be the one leaving instead, and it wasn't long until I was ready to go.

I'd located one of the spare keys I had for Mum's house, always having had at least two keys because keys tend to go missing, so a spare of the spare is handy to have. As it had proven again when the first key I had gone to pick up wasn't where I thought I'd left it, but never mind, I had a backup. Once I had it, there was nothing to do but say my goodbyes to my family, a goodbye that I hoped would be a very short-lived one.

'I'll see you tomorrow,' I'd called to my son through his closed bedroom door. 'I hope you get some sleep.'

There was no response.

'I hope you get some sleep too,' I'd said to Frederik next as we stood by the open front door, both of us peering out into the dark night that I would soon be venturing out into.

'We'll figure this out,' was all he had said to me before we hugged and I left, although crucially, neither one of us told the other that we loved them. Perhaps we should have done, or perhaps we were both afraid that we might not hear it back at that moment in time.

I was glad of the short drive over here, if only to try and clear my head, and now that I'm here, I am hungry. If it's ridiculous to want to eat something in the middle of the night, it's just as ridiculous that I've had to come here. Of course, I'm blaming Haven for this fact as I go into my mother's kitchen and start opening the cupboards to see if there is anything edible I can have.

Anything fresh was thrown out in my first clean, but there are still a few tins in the cupboards, and I find some beans that will do the job of satiating my appetite until a more appropriate time to eat comes around in the morning.

As the beans cook, I wander around the downstairs rooms of my mother's house, but everything looks the same as it did the last time I was here. That's perhaps one of the most unsettling things about a person's home after they have died. Everything just stays frozen in time, as the deceased left it, and unless anyone else comes to make a mess, nothing will change at all. At least I'm here to make a bit of a mess. Once the beans are cooked, I pour them onto a plate and sit down at the kitchen table to eat them.

Dining solo here makes me think of how many mealtimes my mother must have had just like this. Maybe I should have invited her around for meals more often and not been quite as preoccupied with my own busier dinner table. It doesn't matter now. Death removes the option of choice.

I plan to eat my meagre meal and then go upstairs to bed,

but before I can spoon the last few mouthfuls of beans into my mouth, my phone rings.

I am expecting it to be my husband checking that I got here okay, but it's not. It's my son, but not the one I want to hear from the most right now. Rather than Joel calling me at this late hour of the night, it's Scott.

What is he doing awake?

And what does he want?

'Hello?' I say as I answer his call, and he seems as surprised to hear from me as I am from him.

'Why are you not asleep?' he wants to know.

'I could ask you the same question,' I reply plainly as I put the call on speakerphone so I can tidy up while I talk.

'Got a lot on my mind,' my son says as I carry my plate to the sink.

'Like what?'

Scott doesn't answer. Instead, he asks another question.

'Is Joel okay?'

'Why wouldn't he be?' I ask.

'He just posted something online about difficult families.'

That doesn't sound good. But it does sound like something my youngest would do after a family dispute. Can't people just keep things behind closed doors like they did in the old days and not share all sorts of private matters with total strangers? I guess not.

'It's a long story,' I say. 'Come by the house tomorrow and I'll tell you all about it.'

'Is it about Haven?' Scott asks, guessing correctly immediately.

My silence is my answer.

'What has she done?' Scott wants to know. 'What has she said?'

'Nothing worth repeating,' I reply as I twirl my hair tightly around my finger and look at my reflection in the kitchen window.

'Tell me,' Scott says, and I can detect the desperation in his voice, even down the phone line.

'She has made some pretty wild accusations,' I say with a sigh. 'Accusations that relate to your grandmother and how she died.'

'I knew that girl was bad news. I could tell the first time I met her.'

'And you haven't been shy to tell her that, have you?' I say to my son.

'What?'

'I know you have been messaging Haven and warning her away from our family,' I say. 'It all came out tonight, so you don't need to try and deny it.'

'She thinks I hurt Grandma!' Scott cries, incredulous.

'I know she does, and I told her what a stupid belief that is,' I say firmly. 'Don't worry, I kicked her out of my house for saying such a thing and, with any luck, she's gone for good now.'

'You kicked her out?'

'Yes, after an accusation like that, of course I did,' I reply. 'I'm your mother and it's my job to protect my children from anything. That includes awful accusations.'

'You really think she's gone?' Scott asks me, sounding more like a worried little boy than the strong, dependable man I like to think he has grown into.

'Only time will tell,' I say with another sigh. 'But if she has any sense, she'll be long gone. Coming into my home and accusing my eldest child of murder. Who does she think she is? But one thing is for sure. If I ever see her again, she'll find out what murder really looks like.'

TWENTY-EIGHT

HAVEN

If eavesdropping on private conversations was a skill, I could teach it. I've certainly had my fair share of experience over the years and, right now, I'm getting some more practice.

I've heard everything that has been said on the call between Liane and Scott, thanks to her putting her son on speakerphone.

It's a call that is not over yet.

But it might as well be after what I just heard.

Did Liane really say the 'm' word? I'm sure she did and not only that, but she used it in reference to me. *Murder*. Okay, so she might not have been talking literally and only expressing her anger at me accusing her son of the same thing, but it was still a shocking thing to hear. If I had any doubts about Liane's level of hatred towards me, they are well and truly resolved now. It's obvious she never wants to see me again, and the same goes for Scott, who sounded anxious on the call, if such a thing can be detected over the phone.

I have been crouching at the top of the stairs, listening to what was being said below me, but Liane has ended the call now, telling her son to get some sleep, and I can only assume she is going to try and do the same. That means she is going to be coming upstairs very soon and that is a big problem because I'm already up here and will rapidly run out of places to hide if I have company.

But before I move, I think about how Liane didn't ask Scott about the accusations I made against him. She didn't once put the question to her son about whether anything I said was remotely true. She just blindly trusts him, presumably like any mother would, but that doesn't help me very much. Because she didn't ask Scott, he didn't have to deny anything, but at least that might have made him sweat. As it is, he's still getting away with what he has done, and I am increasingly convinced that a murder occurred on this staircase where I lurk now, and not an accident like everyone else assumes.

However, I have something more pressing to worry about at the moment.

Liane is leaving the kitchen.

I think she's coming upstairs next.

I quickly but quietly move away from the staircase and retreat to the bedroom I was trying to sleep in earlier. I have to assume that Liane will visit the bathroom, so I can't hide in there. I also have to hope that when it comes to picking a bedroom to spend the night in, she'll opt for a bigger room than here. This house was her mother's so she should be far more comfortable here than I am. But I'll have to wait and see where she goes.

Once I'm back in the bedroom, I slowly lower myself to the carpet before crawling under the bed. It's dusty under here and I have to stifle a sneeze, but I'm confident I can remain hidden as long as Liane doesn't come in here and start snooping around. If she does, I'm screwed, but maybe I already am anyway.

I hear footsteps on the stairs and now I'm holding my breath, as if that extra thing will make any difference to whether or not I'm caught. I listen as Liane reaches the top of the stairs, and then I hear her flick a light switch.

Light filters through the half-open bedroom door, and next I hear a running tap. She is in the bathroom. But where will she go next?

The thought of her coming in here and getting onto the bed I'm hiding under is a terrifying one. Even if I could remain undetected beneath her, the proximity would surely be too much to handle and I'd end up making a noise that would give my position away. So I just have to hope that isn't put to the test.

I listen as Liane does whatever she needs to do in the bathroom. The light goes off. Then I hear her footsteps crossing the hallway. I grit my teeth as I silently pray that she won't pick this room to go into next.

Another light goes on then and I relax slightly when I realise that she has chosen a different bedroom. I think I'm safe. For now, at least. But the way I see it, I only have two options and neither of them is good. Either I stay hidden here all night and wait for Liane to leave tomorrow before I make my exit too. Or, I wait until Liane falls asleep and try and sneak out of the house then, which seems the far more daunting option of the two.

I wish there was a third option.

But there isn't.

I'm in a mess.

And I have no one to blame for it but myself.

I thought I was being clever by coming here, but now I've gone and got myself trapped and it feels like the only way not to get caught is to spend a sleepless night lying under this bed, waiting for dawn. I can't even risk falling asleep in case I snore or make any kind of noise that could alert Liane. If I did, I would wake up to the sight of a police officer pulling me out from under the bed.

The only thing I can do is listen, so that's what I do as I hear Liane moving around in the bedroom next to this one. Eventually, the light goes off again. All is quiet now, and after several minutes without hearing another sound, I have to assume she is trying to get some sleep. I relax slightly due to the fact that I'm not going to be discovered here anytime soon, but any relief is short-lived. I really don't want to have to lie here all night, but dare I risk leaving my position? In the end, I decide to stay put. Even if I did somehow make it out, I haven't got anywhere to go. At least here, I'm relatively warm and reasonably comfortable. The carpet beats concrete, and a roof over my head, or a bed in this case, beats being totally exposed to the weather outside.

But before I can try and get as comfortable as I can, I hear the sound of a light switch going on. A moment later, I hear footsteps, and suddenly, the bedroom door is opening.

Liane is coming in.

What is she doing? I thought she was asleep. I can hardly ask her what she's up to. All I can do is hold my breath again.

I can see Liane's bare feet now, moving across the carpet so close to my head. If she bent down, she would see me under here, but she's not doing that.

She's doing something almost as bad, though.

She's getting into the bed above me.

I have no idea why Liane just changed her mind about where to sleep and can only assume the first bed she tried didn't feel comfortable enough. But now she is trying this bed, the last bed in the house I wanted her to try, and I am forced to listen to the sound of her wriggling under the duvet above me.

The bed creaks a little as Liane gets into position, and I'm forced to clamp a hand over my mouth through fear of inadvertently making a noise. All it would take is a little air escaping my lips at a higher volume than normal and I would be rumbled. I imagine Liane would scream if she realised there was someone under the bed, before she would go through other states, from shock to anger, all whilst trying to grab hold of me and stop me from getting away.

If only my boyfriend could see me now.

Maybe he would give up on me.

Everything goes quiet above me and it stays that way for a while. I can keep track of the time by looking at the clock on my phone and that's how I'm able to see when it reaches the half-hour mark since Liane last made a sound. She must be asleep. But still I dare not move. I don't move until, just short of forty minutes, I hear a wonderful sound.

Snoring.

Liane is definitely asleep and after that most recent scare, I am most definitely getting out of here while I can.

I roll out from under the bed and slowly get to my feet, keeping my eyes on the still shape on the bed before me. But I don't linger, taking my bag from under the bed where it was hiding with me and sneaking out of the bedroom before creeping down the stairs. Step by step, slowly but surely, creeping towards the front door.

Once I have made it, I use my key to unlock it before stepping outside and then relocking the door, as Liane will expect to find it in the morning. Then I walk away from the house as quickly as I can, not knowing where I'm going, only that it has to be somewhere well away from *her*.

TWENTY-NINE

LIANE

I dream of my family. All of us, together, on a holiday, enjoying some sunshine. I see my boys as youngsters, playing in the pool. I see my husband, lying on a lounger with a beer in his hand. And I see my mother, sitting up in a chair and watching her grandsons with a smile on her face. As for me, I'm happy, and why wouldn't I be when I'm on holiday? Especially a free one. Mum paid for this trip. That's not the only reason she is here with us though. She did offer to give us money for only the four of us to go away, aware that Frederik and I had been saving up to buy a bigger home. But we insisted she come with us if she was paying, so here she is.

I am glad she is here. It's nice to have Mum around.

One day, sadly, that won't be the case.

When I open my eyes, I am very quickly reminded that Mum has gone and my family will always feel different to how it did on that sunny day by the pool many years ago. I suppose it could have been worse. I could have had a nightmare instead of that pleasant dream. I could have had a nightmare about Haven and her wild accusations that threaten to disrupt my family even more than it has already been disrupted since Mum passed. Thankfully, I didn't, so I didn't see Haven in my sleep. With a bit of luck, I won't be seeing her now that my eyes are open either.

I get out of bed, the one in this spare room that I slept in last night after deeming my mother's main bed to be far too uncomfortable for me. I have no idea how Mum slept in that particular bed every night. The mattress felt like it was full of lumps and bumps, although I am aware that everyone has their own preferences and never more so than when it comes to our own beds. But this other bed was comfortable enough for me to achieve a few hours' sleep, and while I let out a yawn as I make my way into the bathroom, I got more rest than I thought I would when I arrived here last night.

I wash and then return to the bedroom to get dressed. But as I do, I notice something on the carpet by the bed. What is that?

Kneeling down, I pick up the item to take a closer look. When I do, I see that it is an earring. Did it belong to my mother? I doubt it because this looks far more fashionable than the type of jewellery she was known to wear. But if not hers then whose? It's definitely not mine. It's not my style at all. But who else does that leave?

I think about it for a moment before she pops into my head again.

Haven.

Could this earring belong to her? I try to think if I have seen her wearing something like this, and the more I think about it, the more I realise I might have. But what is it doing here, on my late mother's carpet?

She was here the other day. She came with Joel to help do some packing. Did she lose it then? Maybe. But I don't remember her being in this room that particular day. But if not then, when?

I decide to keep the earring with me as I finish getting dressed before going downstairs. I won't bother checking the cupboards to see if there's anything for breakfast because even if there is, I don't really want to start my day with food from a tin. That's how I ended yesterday, and I want today to be much better than that, for more reasons than one.

I consider calling Frederik and checking in with him to see what the atmosphere is at our house before I go home. I can't imagine it's great, but my husband might surprise me and give me some good news. He might say something about how Joel has woken up this morning and feels like I reacted appropriately to the situation when I threw his girlfriend out. If so, me and my youngest son don't have to be at war for the foreseeable future. But somehow, I have a feeling it's not going to be as easy as that.

Deciding to hang on to being optimistic rather than realistic, I leave the house, making sure the door is locked before getting into my car and starting the short drive home. As I go, I think about where Haven might be now. Hopefully out of town already if she has any sense. Wherever she spent the night, today is a fresh start for her as well as it is for me, and I hope she is safe, well, but not planning on coming anywhere near any of us again. I also wonder how Scott is after I told him about my confrontation with Haven, when she had openly accused him of murdering his grandmother. My poor boy must be suffering because that's such a heinous thing to be accused of. But he's made of strong stuff, and I suspect he's already at work now, wearing his greasy uniform and fixing another car, doing his best to get on with his life despite somebody trying hard to ruin it.

I don't want to get the police involved in this because that will only add more drama and stress to our lives. But I will if these fabled accusations continue any longer. If Haven has any sense, she will know that pursuing this will result in the police getting involved and I doubt she would want that. That's probably why she hasn't already gone to them herself with her claims against Scott. It's because she knows they won't take her seriously. It's also because she is afraid they might figure out she is the bad one, a fact I've already discovered.

As my house comes into view, it feels strange to be arriving home here so early in the morning. But I'll soon be inside, enjoying a cup of tea in my kitchen, and things will slowly start to get back to normal from there.

I can't wait.

I park and enter my house, eager to get the kettle on and make some breakfast. But as I approach the kitchen door, I hear voices on the other side. I can hear Frederik and Joel, which tells me they are both up already. They don't seem to be arguing, which is a good sign, just like it's a good sign that our son is not hiding away in his bedroom, avoiding his parents. I can only hope the arguing and the avoidance don't start again when I go in.

I open the kitchen door and walk in purposefully, conscious that I don't want it to feel like I am intruding here. But I stop still when I see who is sitting at the breakfast bar.

I already knew my husband and son were in here.

But I didn't know she was here.

I didn't know Haven was back in my house.

But she is.

And she's smiling at me.

THIRTY

HAVEN

'What's going on?' Liane asks when she sees me sitting with her family, enjoying a breakfast of croissants and bagels. I was just about to ask Frederik to pass the butter, but I better wait until his wife gets over the shock of seeing me here.

'Hey, you're back early!' Frederik says as he rises out of his seat and approaches his wife, although she quickly takes a step back from him. But she doesn't take her eyes off me as she does.

'Why is she here?' Liane demands to know, and while it's hardly the best way to say good morning, I choose not to call her out on that. Instead, I just take another bite out of my breakfast.

'I can explain,' Frederik says, sounding like he's a naughty schoolkid who has just been caught doing something he shouldn't and now needs to explain himself to the headmistress.

'How can you explain this?' Liane replies. 'How can you explain letting her back in this house after what she said?'

'Mum, just calm down,' Joel tries, but my boyfriend has clearly underestimated his mother's capability to be in the same room as me again. Unbeknownst to her, we were actually in the same room last night, when I was hiding under the bed she was sleeping in, but again, I don't think this is the time to mention that.

'Haven came back here late last night,' Frederik explains to his wife. 'She showed up on the doorstep at 3 a.m. and said she had nowhere to go. What could I do? Turn her away?'

'Yes, that's exactly what you should have done!' Liane cries.

I am glad that Frederik did not turn me away, although I'm sure the fact that Joel insisted he let me in played a big part in that decision. Whatever the case, I was allowed into this house, and I was glad about that. After the scare at Valerie's house, I didn't have the energy or mental capacity to take another risk elsewhere. I just needed a warm bed. I needed my boyfriend. And he needed to ask me something very important.

'How could you think that my brother killed her?' Joel asked me once I was in his bedroom and the door was firmly closed. 'I just don't understand it.'

'Maybe I'm wrong, but it's just a feeling I have,' I'd replied. 'I know you love your brother, but you have been away in Australia having the time of your life while he has been here, trying to keep a struggling business going. I know he pretends he is successful, but he's not, and debt and desperation can drive anybody to do terrible things.'

'I just can't see it,' Joel had said, shaking his head from where he sat on the edge of the bed. 'Not my brother. He's not a killer.'

'He's threatened me,' I went on. 'I have the proof and it shows he is not the nice guy everyone thinks he is. But I admit I don't have any evidence that he pushed your grandmother down the stairs, other than him arranging to be there on the day she died. So I understand if you want me to stop this and leave.'

'No, I don't want you to leave,' Joel had said, reaching out for my hand and showing me that while he was incredibly conflicted about what I was accusing his brother of, he still wanted to be with me too. I wanted the same, so we spent the night together, sleeping side by side, and I was feeling a little better about things when I woke up. I was feeling a little better until Liane came home.

'I can't believe this,' she says, looking at her husband as if he has made a very grave mistake. 'I cannot believe you have allowed that spiteful little witch back into this house.'

'Dad did the right thing,' Joel says then. 'He made sure Haven was safe and that we all got some sleep.'

'Fine, you got some sleep. Now get out,' Liane says, pointing at me and my croissant as I'm mid-bite.

'Look, I'm sure this is all one big misunderstanding, and I think if the two of you could just talk, I'm sure we could sort this out,' Frederik says.

'I'd like to talk,' I say then, speaking up for the first time since Liane entered this kitchen that was so calm and peaceful only a moment ago. Frederik hadn't exactly been warm to me, but was being polite, no doubt treading delicately because he doesn't want to lose his youngest son over this. But I can see it won't be easy with Liane.

'You've done enough talking,' she says to me. 'I don't want to hear another lie that comes out of your mouth.'

'I'm not here to lie,' I say, holding up my hands.

'Really? Let's put that to the test then,' Liane says, stepping forward before taking a seat opposite me at the breakfast bar. 'Look my son right in the eyes now and tell him that you are not only here for his inheritance money.'

'She doesn't need to do that,' Joel tries.

'Yes, she does,' Liane snaps back. 'Do it.'

I can see that Liane thinks she has put me in a very uncomfortable position, but the reality is I have no problem turning to look at my boyfriend and saying what she told me to say. So I do just that.

'I am not here for your inheritance money, I promise. I'm here because I love you.'

Joel smiles.

'I know,' he says before looking back at his mum. 'Just like I know that it's time for me and Haven to leave here.'

'What? Where will you go?' Liane cries.

'We're buying an apartment in the city,' Joel tells her, discussing the topic that Joel and I spent time talking about while we were lying in bed last night after I had been allowed back into this house. The two of us realised we couldn't continue to see each other here, so we needed a plan. Now we have one.

'We're going to use the money Grandma has given me to get a place and then you won't have to see us anymore,' Joel says.

'That's not what we want. Tell him, Liane,' Frederik implores his wife, but she stays silent, which tells us what she really thinks.

'Whatever,' Joel says before standing up. 'Come on, Haven. Let's get out of here.'

I follow my boyfriend out of the kitchen and upstairs to his bedroom, where he puts his things into a bag. My bag is already packed, so it won't take long for us both to be on our way. Neither Liane nor Frederik come upstairs to try and convince us to stay, though I can hear them having a heated argument in the kitchen, so I guess they are preoccupied enough. The atmosphere in this house is terrible, so I can't wait to leave it behind, and once Joel is packed, there is nothing standing in our way. But just before we walk out the door, I need to be absolutely certain that he is doing the right thing.

'I don't want you to choose between me and your family,' I say to him, taking his hand. 'So if you don't want to do this, I understand.'

'I just want you,' he says, and with that, our next move is decided.

We both go downstairs, each carrying our bags, and we can both hear that the argument is continuing in the kitchen. With one look, we both agree that it's best to not interrupt it, so we sneak out of the house and walk away before Joel calls a taxi.

As we anticipate its arrival, the plan is for us to go to a hotel, before possibly renting somewhere while we wait for the inheritance money from his grandmother's savings to eventually reach his bank account. As soon as it does, we can start looking for a proper place to live, a place we will own and a place that we don't have to share with anybody else.

But despite these plans that I should be excited about, I am still worried.

I'm worried that Joel is giving up his family for me.

More than that, I'm worried that his family will do anything to get him back, which would mean getting rid of me.

How would they do that?

I'm sure Scott has an idea.

After all, he knows how to get rid of people...

THIRTY-ONE

SCOTT

'Damn it!' I cry before throwing the wrench at the wall across the garage.

It lands with a loud clatter on the concrete floor and I stare at it as if that tool is the reason for my bad mood today. But of course it isn't. If anything, a trusty wrench is something that usually brings me comfort and solace from the struggles of the outside world. But not today. Nothing can make me feel better about what is going on in my life outside of this garage where I spend so much of my time fixing cars.

I wheel myself out from under the latest vehicle that I've been working on before grabbing a hand towel and wiping off some of the oil on my hands. It's largely a futile task because I spend all day covered in oil, so I won't be fully clean until I have a shower later tonight. I toss the useless towel to the workbench at the side and wipe my hands on my stained overalls, then go to retrieve the wrench from where it lies.

Losing my temper is not an uncommon trait for me. I've always been tightly wound, even if I have done a reasonably good job of keeping that side of myself from other people. I tend to reserve my outbursts of anger for here, in this garage, where I am mostly alone. But recently, my anger has been getting harder to control.

Things have been hard. Money is not easy to come by. Costs are rising and people are trying to save what they can. That leaves business owners like me being squeezed from both ends. Having an increasingly expensive mechanic business to run with an ever-dwindling supply of customers is not a healthy combination. But I should be happier now. I've gained an inheritance that should take all of the pressure off me. I can pay my bills, buy some new tools and still have enough money left over to treat myself to a few personal items. My grandmother's money sure will come in handy around here. But will the price I have to pay to spend it be worth it?

I wish I could work. I wish I could concentrate. But as I pick up the wrench, I know it's only a matter of time until I throw it to the floor again. How can I complete my tasks here when all I can think about is how my grandmother really died?

Valerie didn't deserve what happened to her. But it happened and I thought it could stay secret. But now Haven is here, putting ideas in people's heads, pointing the finger at me, threatening to destroy everything. If only my brother had never met her. If only he was still single then she wouldn't be a problem. Or if she was just as naïve and well-wishing as everybody else who thinks that my grandmother just fell down the stairs in an accident.

But she isn't.

She's smarter than that.

Haven might be right that Valerie was murdered, but I'm hardly going to congratulate her on her powers of deduction and offer to drive her to the police station so she can share her story with them. Instead, I have to hope that she will just leave me and my family alone, as I have already told her to do more than once. If she would just listen then everyone could be okay. I wouldn't have to worry about my life, and she wouldn't have to worry about hers. We could all just move on and pretend none of this ever happened. But I have a feeling that isn't going to happen and that's why I can't stop worrying about the police getting involved and what life would be like for me behind bars.

I would not do well as a caged animal. I cannot go to prison. I need to be free.

Pushing those thoughts out of my head as best as I can, I push myself back under the car. I resume work, using the wrench in the way it was intended to be used. This is a skilful tool, not just something to be thrown around. I feel bad for mistreating it. I also feel bad for mistreating others. But I can't change the past. I can only try and live with it.

I know my parents are on my side, supporting me against Haven's accusations. I hope my brother is too, although I appreciate he is in a very difficult position. But even with my family, it feels like I am on my own here.

This is a mess of my own doing.

So maybe I'm the only one who can fix it.

But just like this car, it's not going to be easy.

THIRTY-TWO

LIANE

I stare at the earring in my hand, the one I found on the bedroom floor in my mother's house and, as of now, the only thing of Haven's that remains here after she and my son left this morning. I could throw it somewhere. Anywhere. But I am holding onto it. I guess it's symbolic. I'm holding onto it because I know it's not the last I've seen of Haven. Not at all.

'How are you feeling?' Frederik asks me as we walk side by side in the park he suggested we go to after the drama of the morning. After being shocked to see Haven in my house and then having a heated argument with my husband while Joel and Haven left, it was obvious I needed a break. So Frederik suggested we come here, to the leafy surroundings of this green space for a bit of fresh air.

I put the earring in my pocket. I haven't mentioned to my husband that this is the same park where I met Haven's brother. I hardly think mentioning something like that is going to cheer either of us up or prevent us from having another argument. So I'll continue to keep it to myself. I really don't want to argue with Frederik. He is my best friend as well as my husband, and I need his support. I need it now more than ever.

'A little bit better,' I say in answer to his question. It's not really the truth. I don't feel any better. But I don't want Frederik to think his suggestion to go for a walk has been a complete waste of time either.

'I think you should talk to somebody,' he says then as we keep walking. 'A therapist, maybe, or a counsellor. Somebody who can help you process the shock of your mother's death.'

'Is that all I talk about with them?' I ask with a sigh. 'Or would I mention Haven too, and how she thinks our eldest son is a killer?'

'Maybe just start with the grief thing and see how it goes,' Frederik says, and we both can't help but laugh at that.

If only life was as simple as a walk in the park. Wouldn't it be wonderful? But we both know it's not, which is why we can laugh here but will soon be reminded of the grim reality when we get home to find Joel gone.

'I don't want to lose us,' I admit then, which is also perhaps an admittance that I have been hard to live with in recent times.

'Me neither,' Frederik replies, and that's comforting to hear.

'And I don't want to lose our sons,' I add. 'But I fear that this woman is trying to take them from us. If she has her way, Joel will never speak to us again and Scott will be in prison for something he didn't do.'

'Nobody is going to prison,' Frederik says calmly. 'Your mother died in an accident and only Haven is suggesting otherwise. Not anybody else and certainly not the police. We don't know why she is making up these false stories about Scott, but they won't lead anywhere. They certainly won't lead to our family breaking up. I promise you that.'

'How can you promise it?' I ask anxiously. 'How can you know for sure that this situation isn't going to get worse, not better?'

'Because I'll see to it that it doesn't get any worse,' Frederik says, pausing and turning to look at me. I stop walking too and we stand face to face on the park path, staring into one another's eyes, totally undistracted by any other people who pass us.

'I have a bad feeling about this,' I admit to my husband. 'I can't shake it.'

Frederik lets out a sigh, but I'm not paranoid. My fears are entrenched in something very real.

'I know Scott didn't hurt his grandmother and it's insane for someone to suggest it,' I say. 'But if Haven's accusation about Scott gets to the police, I fear they will take it seriously based on what he did in the past.'

Frederik knows exactly what I am talking about.

'No,' he says. 'That was a long time ago and it was completely different.'

'It was violent conduct and it could be used as proof that he has a temper and is prone to outbursts of violence.'

'It was a drunken fight outside a pub when he was eighteen years old,' Frederik cries. 'He wasn't the first young guy to drink one too many beers and end up in a fight, and he won't be the last.'

'But he got a criminal record. He punched someone who ended up in hospital. Scott was charged. Yes, he didn't go to prison, but there will be a record of it, and it will come up if Haven gives the police a reason to look at him again.'

'No self-respecting police officer is going to think that somebody who has a fight outside with his mates when he was a teenager is then capable of murder ten years later. Scott, like most people, was a fool at eighteen. But now he is a grown-up, hard-working, respected member of society and that's what the police will care about, which is why they will dismiss this silly notion that he is a murderer, just like we have already done.'

I want to believe my husband. I want to believe it could be as easy as that. But the fact is, Scott is not perfect. He made a mistake in the past, albeit a drunken mistake that some other men his age might make, and while nobody died, he can't claim to have a flawless history. I hope Haven doesn't know about it or it would only strengthen her resolve in thinking that Scott is a bad guy. But surely Joel hasn't told her what his older brother did a decade ago. It's barely worth mentioning. We've all moved on, Scott in particular. He's more ashamed than anybody that he once got so drunk that he punched someone and they needed the care of a paramedic. He is not that guy anymore and he is certainly not a murderer.

'I just want this to be over,' I say to my husband as we start walking again.

'I know,' he replies. 'Hopefully it will be.'

With no way of knowing that for sure, we complete the rest of our walk in worried silence. Meanwhile, Haven is out there somewhere, with my youngest son, probably living her best life as they discuss what to spend the inheritance money on.

That young woman is wreaking havoc wherever she goes.

What will she do next?

THIRTY-THREE

HAVEN

A hotel room is usually a place for a person to relax. But that doesn't really apply to me as I enter the room where me and my boyfriend are due to stay for a couple of nights.

'This is great!' Joel cries as he admires the double bed, spacious bathroom and the large flatscreen TV on the wall. 'I could get used to this.'

'I'm sure the credit card company could get used to it too,' I say, reminding him that we are only here because he used a credit card to fund it. But it's not a problem because he'll have £75,000 very soon, although I still think we should be wise with money, where we can be. That's why I object to his idea that we order a bottle of champagne to the room.

'Spoilsport,' Joel says before taking off his T-shirt. 'I'm going to test the shower in here. You want to join me?'

'I think I'm just going to try and rest for a minute,' I say, looking at the bed.

'Suit yourself,' Joel replies before disappearing into the bathroom.

I hear the shower turn on and, within seconds, Joel is whistling. He seems content, far more content than I thought he would be, given his delicate family situation right now. How is he able to separate all of that from his mind and find some peace? I would have thought he would be cut up about the rift that was developing between us and his parents, never mind the potential issue of his brother and him being at war if Joel stays on my side.

I get onto the bed and do what I told Joel I was aiming to do. I try to relax. But it doesn't work, not even after turning the TV on and trying to distract myself with something on there. By the time Joel emerges from the bathroom with a towel wrapped around his waist, only one of us looks like we are refreshed.

'You look tired,' he says as he walks to my side of the bed and gives me a kiss on the head. 'I was thinking I might go out for a walk. Maybe grab a beer somewhere. How about you stay here and rest? I could be back in about an hour and a half. How does that sound?'

It actually sounds quite good. I could do with some time to myself. I'll get off the bed at some point and have a shower and maybe I'll be feeling better when Joel returns.

'That sounds like a plan,' I say, forcing a smile onto my face.

Joel gets dressed as I watch some more TV, and by the time he is ready to go, I am feeling lazy but settled.

'I'll be back soon,' he says, giving me another kiss. 'Then we'll get some food.'

I am hungry so the prospect of a meal is inviting, but right now, this bed and a warm shower at some point are even more inviting, so I wave my boyfriend off before snuggling further into my pillow.

I guess Joel wants a walk to clear his head and that is a good thing. He's most likely checking his bank account at regular intervals too, to see if the inheritance money has gone into his account. It should be anytime now and I'm sure the moment it shows up will be a moment full of conflicting emotions. Sadness that he gained this money from the death of a loved one. But excitement about how the money could be used to fund the next part of his life.

It wasn't my idea to get him to spend the money on a place for us to live. I would never tell him how to spend his inheritance, and I certainly knew that making any suggestions would run the risk of drawing Liane's ire. Particularly if that suggestion had been to spend the cash on a city-centre apartment that I got to live in too. But the idea of the apartment is all Joel's, and it does make sense that our next step would be to move into our own place together. We are sticking around here rather than returning to travelling, and we are sticking together, despite what his mother might want. But there is no respite from my paranoia because I know that at some point, I'll have to see *him* again.

Scott. The man I think is a murderer. I can't avoid him forever. He'll pop up again somewhere. I can't expect him not to. He'll want to see his brother. There will be some kind of family occasion, whatever it might be, so this isn't going to get any easier. But going to the police will only make it harder, so I'm stuck in the middle.

Right now, I'm nothing but a woman with a conspiracy theory.

I eventually make it off the bed and into the shower and it feels good to have the strong jets of water hitting my aching body. I still feel stiff from my exploits last night in which I had to squeeze myself under a bed and stay there for far longer than I wanted to, but the warm water is soothing my aches and pains.

After the shower, I wrap a warm towel around my wet body and take a good look at myself in the mirror. The toll of the last few days is plain to see. It's written all over my face, from the bags under my eyes to the wrinkles on my forehead that I could have sworn were not there before. It's not anything that a bit of make-up can't conceal, but still, as I stand here and stare at myself, I hardly look like someone who is capable of standing up to anyone who wants to shut me up.

That's why I better be careful.

I can't allow myself to be alone with Scott if the situation ever arose.

I can't give him the chance to silence me like he silenced Valerie.

I dry my hair, then go back into the bedroom to get dressed. But I've not even removed my tightly wrapped towel from around my body when I hear a knock at the door.

Who could that be? Joel back already and having to knock after forgetting his room key? Or an employee of the hotel coming here to check everything is okay with our stay? Maybe Joel did go ahead and order something from room service, perhaps a treat for me while he is gone. I wouldn't put it past him, so as I make my way to the door, I have a smile on my face at the prospect of being greeted by a big bottle of champagne or some tasty snacks. But then I open the door and my smile instantly dissolves. That's because it's not room service. Instead, it's the last thing I wanted to see.

Scott is here.

And now my biggest fear just came true.

I am alone with him.

THIRTY-FOUR

SCOTT

THIRTY MINUTES EARLIER

We need to talk.

That was the simple message that I received from my brother at lunchtime and the message that has led to me being here, at this hotel in the city centre. I should be back at my garage now, still wearing my overalls and still covered in grease. Instead, I am here, in this plush building, wearing a white shirt and black jeans, and I am here because of one important thing.

I love my brother.

That's why I have to hear what he has to say for himself.

I spot my sibling seated at a table in the hotel bar, two beers in front of him, in preparation for my arrival. Of course he knows what I like to drink. It's the same thing he likes to drink. Our taste for beer is just one of the many things we have in common. I once thought we had the same taste in women too, based on the appearances of the various females that have frequented our lives in the past.

But I don't think that anymore.

I stopped thinking that the moment I realised my brother's latest girlfriend was a threat.

'Hey,' Joel says when he sees me approaching and he stands up before holding out his hand for me to shake.

If it seems like a very rigid, formal introduction for two brothers to take part in, I think that too, which is why I decline to offer my own hand. Usually, we would hug, or slap one another on the back, or simply smile, shrug and start teasing one another. But given the current circumstances that our relationship exists in, I don't do any of those other things.

I just sit down and have a sip of my beer.

'Okay,' Joel says as he retakes his seat. 'So I guess you're mad at me.'

'Oh, I don't know, bro. Have a guess. Your girlfriend is running around telling everyone that I killed Grandma and, as far as I can tell, you're still with her, so yeah, I guess I am a little mad at you.'

'Haven isn't running around telling everyone that you killed Grandma,' Joel tries to correct me, but I just laugh sarcastically.

'Sorry, you're right. She's only told you, Mum and Dad so far, so just the closest people in the world to me, so that makes it all better, doesn't it?'

Joel has never appreciated my sarcasm, and it doesn't look like he is going to start now.

'We need to sort this out,' Joel says, picking up his beer. 'We need to figure out a way for things to go back to normal between us all.'

'That's easy. Get rid of her,' I say simply.

'I'm not going to do that. I love Haven.'

'Wow, I always thought I was the smarter one out of the two of us, but now you are really proving it. How can you love a woman who accuses your own brother of murder?'

'Look, I get it, you're upset. I would be too if someone thought I had done something crazy. I don't know where Haven has got the idea from, but she is stubborn, and once something is in her head, I've found that the best thing to do is to just let it run its course before she gets bored and moves onto something else.'

'Gets bored? So she's threatening to blow up my whole life because she's bored?' I cry, throwing my hands up in the air.

'No, that's not what I'm saying. What I mean is Haven needs to realise in her own time that her idea of you killing Grandma is a false one and, once she does, I am sure she will apologise and feel bad about all of this.'

'You're sure, are you? What if that doesn't happen? What if she goes to the police?'

'She won't.'

'But what if she does?' I repeat, my voice loud enough to attract the attention of a few other patrons of this bar, who all look over with differing levels of disdain on their faces.

'Then you'll be fine because you have absolutely nothing to hide, right?' Joel asks me.

'Of course I have nothing to hide!' I lie. 'But it's not as simple as that. What if the police don't believe me? What if they see that I have a criminal record?'

'That guy you punched outside a pub when you were eighteen? That's hardly relevant to anything.'

'Yes, it is! It could be used against me. If Haven says I am violent, that only proves her point!'

Again, some of the people in the bar look over in my direction and, again, they don't seem impressed with me.

'You don't have to worry about any of that because Haven isn't going to go to the police,' Joel assures me. 'Seriously, this will all blow over soon, I'm sure of it.'

I stare at my sibling and wish I was blessed with his innocence.

'I love you, but you are so naïve,' I say with a sad shake of my head.

We share an awkward silence then as we both sip our beers, and I'm sure it is a silence that is appreciated by the other people in the bar.

'So what are you doing here?' I ask when I'm finally ready for more conversation.

'We needed to get out of Mum and Dad's house,' Joel replies.

'We?'

'Me and Haven.'

'She's here?' I ask, looking around in shock.

'Don't worry, she's not in the bar,' Joel tells me. 'She's upstairs. We've got a room in this hotel.'

My brother might just be making conversation, but there's no way I can go back to chatting now that I know that *she* is here. That's because I only want to talk to her now. I just have to figure out a way to get to her.

'How about another beer?' I suggest to Joel. 'But considering your girlfriend is crazy, you can buy them.'

'Fair enough,' Joel says with a laugh as he goes to get up.

'Hey, isn't this the hotel that has the fancy room keycards?' I ask him before he can go.

'Huh?'

'I read an article about it. How the keycards are gold and they have some cool microchip inside them that lights up when you tap them on the doors. I'm sure this is the place. Is it true?'

'I don't think so,' Joe replies, frowning.

'Let me see the card,' I say, gesturing for him to take his room key out of his pocket and, sure enough, he does that.

'See, it's not even gold,' he tells me as he flashes me the card. But in doing so, he also flashes me the number that is written on the paper pouch that the card is in.

414

'I must be mixed up with somewhere else,' I say with a shrug. 'Never mind.'

Joel rolls his eyes then turns to head to the bar.

'I'm just going to go to the toilet,' I call after him. 'Make sure there's a beer here for when I get back.'

Joel gives me the thumbs up as I stand and head to the toilets. But after checking that my brother isn't watching me, I take a detour towards a staircase.

Ascending the stairs, I look out for the sign for the fourth floor and when I find it, I then look for the door with the same number on it as the number that was on my brother's room card.

414

Here it is.

Haven is behind this door.

Now it's time to say hello.

THIRTY-FIVE

HAVEN

PRESENT

I try to close the door, but Scott reaches out a strong hand and prevents me from doing so.

That only leaves me with one other option.

I start backing away from him.

'How did you find me?' I cry. 'What do you want?'

'Hello to you too,' Scott says as he steps into the room before closing the door behind himself.

I wish Joel was here now. I wish he'd never gone out for a walk. Most of all, I wish I hadn't answered the knock at the door.

'Stay away from me,' I say. I grab a pen from the small desk in this room. 'Stay away from me or I'll hurt you with this!'

I hold up the pen so he can see that I have a weapon, although I'm not sure it's one that he deems worthy of staying away from. I guess not because he keeps slowly advancing towards me.

'I just want to talk,' Scott says as he takes small steps closer.

'And you're very good at talking, aren't you, Haven? You're something of an expert in it.'

I keep backing away but I'm going to run out of space soon.

'You've been telling my family that I'm a murderer,' he goes on. 'That's not very nice, is it?'

'Just get out now or I'll call the police!'

'Call the police? Attack me with a pen? Which one is it? Make your mind up.'

Scott sniggers then and this must be what it feels like to be face to face with a cold-blooded killer and have nowhere to go. I've seen this same fate befall countless characters on TV shows over the years, but now it seems it is my turn to experience this and, worst of all, this is not fiction.

As my back bumps into the wall, I know I cannot retreat any further. All I can do now is raise my hand with the pen in it and prepare to strike as soon as Scott gets too close. But he stops and stares at me. Why? What is he doing? Toying with me? Playing with his prey? Savouring the situation for several more seconds?

'You have to stop this,' he says simply, not looking at the poised pen but right into my eyes. 'I'm not going to waste my breath telling you that I'm innocent because you have clearly already made your mind up about that. But what I have to do is warn you that if you don't let this go, things can get a lot worse for you. I don't want that and I'm sure you don't either, so drop this and we can all move on. Trust me, it is for the best.'

As I process what Scott just said to me, I realise he is offering me a chance to make it out of this hotel room alive. That is not a chance I thought I would get when he barged his way in here and started walking towards me. But now that he is giving me a chance, I'd be an idiot not to take it. Wouldn't I?

'Okay, I'll do what you want,' I say, conceding because what other choice do I have in this situation? Agree and live, or disagree and die?

'Thank you,' Scott says, letting out a relieved sigh.

'But you have to admit to me that I was right,' I say. 'Admit what you did. Admit that you killed that poor woman who loved and trusted you and you did it for nothing more than money.'

If it seems like a bad idea to potentially bait the murderous man in front of me, it's too late to worry about that because I've already gone and done it. But I have to. I can't just give him everything he wants without making him admit to his guilt and do battle with whatever conscience he has, for a few seconds, at least.

'I'm not admitting that,' Scott says, shaking his head, and he looks horrified that I would even suggest it. But that only makes me more determined to get him to do this.

'Why not? It's just the two of us in here. I'm not recording anything either,' I say, pointing to where my phone lies on the bedside table. 'Check it. There's no hidden cameras or anything. I had no idea you were coming here. So this is just between us two.'

'Why do you need to hear me say it?' Scott asks.

'I just do,' I reply. 'I just need to know that I've not been imagining things.'

Scott stares at me and I'm wondering if he is close to giving me what I want. Of course, hearing him confess to murder right in front of me is not really what I want, but it is what I need if I am to be able to stop myself from spending the rest of my life second-guessing all of this.

'I can't do it,' Scott eventually says.

'Because you're a coward,' I say to him in disgust.

'No, I'm not,' he snaps back, and I see a fire behind his eyes at my suggestion. That 'C' word seems to have ignited something in him. Maybe that's the button I need to press to get him to confess. Or maybe I would be foolish to anger him anymore.

'You're a coward who killed your grandmother and you hate the fact that I am the one person who has seen through you,' I go on, baiting him further. 'I'm the one person who looks at you in disgust while everyone else just thinks you're this nice guy who works hard running his own business. You hate it, but it's a fact. I know exactly who you are and I always will.'

I should have shut up talking a long time ago, but I didn't and, as Scott steps towards me, I fear I have made a grave error in angering him to this point. As he pushes me back against the wall, I consider screaming. This might be the last chance I get before he wraps his hands around my throat and squeezes the life out of me.

But I don't scream and he doesn't strangle me.

Instead, I notice something very unexpected.

Scott has tears in his eyes.

He doesn't look angry. He looks upset. He doesn't seem strong now either. He seems weak.

Bizarrely, I realise he isn't holding on to me because he wants to hurt me.

He is holding on to me for support.

'What is it?' I ask him, afraid that this could be even worse than anything I had imagined. As Scott lets go of me, I see tears rolling down his cheeks.

What has caused this burly man to break down right in front of me? It can't be all down to what I have said, can it? It can't just be guilt over what he has done, surely?

There is something else. Something more. *Something worse?*

'I did not kill my grandmother,' Scott says as he takes a seat on the edge of the bed and wipes his eyes. 'I loved her. I didn't visit her as often as I should have, but I did love her and I did not hurt her.'

I don't know what to do now so I choose to say nothing and wait for Scott to speak again.

'You couldn't just leave it alone, could you?' Scott goes on, growing increasingly distressed. 'You couldn't just think she fell down the stairs like everyone else thinks.'

'I don't know what is happening here, but I think you should leave,' I say, but I already know it's not going to be as simple as that.

'No, I can't leave here with you thinking I'm a murderer,' Scott says. 'It's not fair.'

I have a sudden crisis of confidence then. Have I got this all wrong? Is Scott actually innocent?

'You are wrong about me,' he says, looking up at me through red-rimmed eyes. 'But you are right about something.'

'What?' I ask anxiously.

'My grandmother was murdered,' he says. 'But I wasn't the one who killed her.'

'Then who?' I ask, prepared for whatever bombshell might be about to come my way.

But nothing could have prepared me for the truth.

Nothing could have prepared me for finding out who the real killer is in this family.

THIRTY-SIX

LIANE

PRESENT – VALERIE'S HOUSE

No self-respecting killer should return to the scene of the crime. But that's what I do every time I come back to my mother's house.

As I re-enter the home where I pushed Mum down the stairs, I don't linger in the specific place where she died. Instead, I walk right past it and get on with what I came here to do. The sooner I have sorted, tidied and packed all the things in here, the sooner this house can be sold and then I'll never have to set foot in it again. The sooner I'll have the money from the sale sitting in my bank account. The sooner mine and Frederik's lives will become far better than they were when Valerie was alive.

As I get to work in the dining room, where I am sorting through the lifetime of paperwork that my mother amassed and stored in the large cupboard in here, I know this is merely a means to an end. It might seem like a very boring task, and it is, but it's still a far simpler task than the one that led me to having to be here today to do this.

The hardest part of this whole plan was always going to be the part where I had to become a murderer.

As I sift through decades of documents that my mother had no need to hang on to, from bank statements to junk mail, I can't help but think about the day I came to this house and ended my mother's life. It was a day that had started like so many others, in that it had started with my husband's alarm clock waking me up early because we had to go to work. I'd never been a fan of Frederik and his early starts, his requirement to rise at dawn so he could get to his workplace for another day and avoid being fired by his boss. Then again, I was hardly a fan of my workplace either. I'd grown bitter and resentful over the years at hearing the sound of that damn alarm cutting through my dreams, stirring me from my sleep, especially after decades of bad sleep due to raising our two children. Scott and Joel had grown and moved out, yet still I was forced into awakening at sunrise and drudging through every day in a sleepy fog of fatigue, and it was all because my husband and I had jobs to go to.

I'd long grown weary of working, but with a mortgage still to pay, one son in Australia who often called for extra funds and another son who had a mechanic business that was struggling to keep going, there was no end in sight. That was even before any potential grandchildren arrived on the scene and squeezed our finances further. Despite loving the idea of grandchildren one day, and the possibility of taking them out for fun days that involved lots of ice cream and trips to the toy store, I knew it would all be tainted if I was still worrying about money in those golden years. But how could it not? Both Frederik and I were begrudgingly forced to face the fact that we'd both likely be working into our late sixties before we reached the age for a state pension in the UK, if not beyond. That meant no time for ourselves other than on weekends, no spontaneous trips or getting to see the world we had missed out on seeing in our youth and, worst of all, many more years of being woken up by alarm clocks.

Neither of us liked it, but what choice did we have? Frederik accepted our situation with his usual humour. But I didn't accept it. I hated it, and I hated it more and more every day. But perhaps the main reason I hated it was because I knew there was one person who could help us get out of this situation. It was a person who had already escaped the drudgery of work and was spending her time doing whatever she wanted. A person who had more money than she needed but was keeping tight control over it until the day that she died.

My mother.

As I throw away more useless pieces of paperwork, I still resent how Mum had so much money yet didn't share it with her family while she was alive. Sure, she helped out occasionally, giving cash to her grandkids on their birthdays or at Christmas, or treating Frederik and me to a meal out every now and again. There was that one time she paid to take us all on holiday too, which was a nice getaway, but only reinforced all my other problems when I came back home to them and returned to work. Despite the occasional lavish gifts, none of it made an inherently tangible difference to our lives, and it would have been so much better if Mum could have passed on some of her wealth much sooner in a more meaningful way. Instead of taking us on a simple holiday and giving us an all-too-brief respite from our stresses and strains, she could have gifted me and Frederik all that money to make our day-to-day lives easier permanently. What my mother failed to see was that beneficiaries don't always need their inheritance when we're older because by that time we've already been working for decades, raised our families and paid off our mortgages. We need it earlier, when the kids are young, when the bills are still high and when the pressure of work is weighing us down every day. Gifting us a sum of money then would have made it all so much easier, not gifting it when we're old and grey, by which point we don't have as much time to spend it or many things left to spend it on.

I dropped this hint to my mother on several occasions throughout my thirties and forties, explaining to her how difficult life was for Frederik and me and how we were being squeezed financially from every direction. But all she would do was say the same damn thing.

'Don't worry about money. You'll have plenty of it when I'm gone.'

Yes, I knew that Mum would leave me and my family hundreds of thousands of pounds in her will and yes, I was very grateful for that. But she just couldn't see that it would have been far less useful to me at seventy than it would be at fifty. If my mother ended up living into her nineties, I would already have spent my entire life working, so what good is a bundle of cash then when my best years are behind me? How about sharing some of it when me and my husband still had each other, our relative youth and our health to enjoy it with?

Mum never saw it that way. 'You and Frederik will live to a grand old age and there will be plenty of time for you to do all the things you want to do in retirement, just like there is for me now,' she would say whenever I was moaning to her about my soulless, time-sucking job. Such a sentiment only made me grow more frustrated as more and more time slipped away, and it overshadowed all the time I was around her.

Visiting her at home, something that felt more like an obligation and a sense of duty to my late father than anything I wanted to do, became more difficult. It felt like Mum was either totally oblivious to my daily drudgery and desire to escape it or she was fully aware of it and taking some sort of pleasure in it, as if she felt the next generation had to work just as hard as she had for her money. I told her more than once that the world had changed a lot since she was my age. Things were a lot more expensive these days, from mortgages to childcare costs to simply filling up your basket at the grocery store, and wages hadn't risen in line with those costs. Some of these discussions led to arguments and some of them took place in front of our other family members, which was regrettable, but arguments aren't always avoidable, are they?

But most of the time, Mum either brushed over my concerns or ignored them completely, sparing us another argument but not helping my predicament in the slightest.

While Mum could ignore it, I couldn't ignore the growing sense of frustration that was burning in my belly.

It got bigger and bigger, but I didn't know what to do with it.

Until I woke up in the middle of the night with an idea.

What if I sped up the process of getting my inheritance?

What if my husband and I didn't have to work for another twenty years before we got to enjoy life?

What if I hastened my mother's demise?

Once the terrible idea was in my head, it was impossible to shake. It stayed there, burrowing its way deeper into my brain. Every time I yawned, or my husband yawned. Every time our direct debits left our bank account. Every time one of us had our holiday request denied by our employer. Every time I got another day older and longed for the alternative life I could be living.

Every alarm clock. Every commute. Every cleaning job. Every sink I scrubbed and every floor I mopped. Every lunch break that went too fast. Every Monday morning that went too slow.

Until it all became too much and I decided the time for thinking about it was over.

The time for action had arrived.

I knew I would have to make it look like an accident. But I also knew that was possible because my mother lived alone and she was in her mid-seventies. Would anybody really think it was strange if she fell down the stairs?

I doubted it.

So I just had to do it.

On the day I did, I arrived at my mother's house with a simple knock on the door. The nerves I carried inside myself were concealed by my false smile when Mum answered and said she was surprised to see me. I was supposed to be at work. I told her I was on my lunch hour. A simple lie to get closer. Mum believed it. Why wouldn't she? She invited me in. Again, why wouldn't she? I glanced at the staircase as I entered. All I had to do was get her to the top of it. Such a dark thought was offset by reminding myself that my mother had ignored all my pleas or hints for financial help over the years and seemed to take some perverse pleasure in my struggles. But very soon, the perverse pleasure would be all mine.

'Sorry, can I just use the bathroom?' I asked as nonchalantly as I could.

'Of course, dear,' Mum said. 'I'll put the kettle on.'

I went up the stairs and lingered at the top for a moment, composing myself, knowing the time was almost here. But there was still time to change my mind. To back out. To not try and kill my mother.

It would have been easy to alter my plan. To go back downstairs, have a cup of tea with Mum and then leave as if it was just another day. But then I thought of all the early mornings I still had ahead of me if I didn't do this. All the alarm clocks. All the cleaning. All the bills to be paid. All the overdraft reminders from my bank whenever my funds dipped slightly too low. And most importantly, all the life I was missing out on living if everything stayed the same.

Then I called out to my mother.

'Mum, what's this smell up here?'

'What?' she called back.

'There's a strange smell.'

'Is there?'

I heard Mum leaving the kitchen and approaching the stairs.

'I'm not sure where it's coming from,' I said, knowing that would only entice her to come up here and join in my investigation.

I was proven right, and as Mum came up the stairs, I took a deep breath.

When Mum reached the top of the stairs, I rushed towards her with my arms outstretched and despite her locking eyes with me, I didn't stop what I was doing.

When Mum fell back down the stairs, I already knew it was too late. I already knew the deed was done and there was no saving her then. The only thing I didn't know was whether my mother would die in this fall or if I would have to finish her off after it.

As she tumbled down the stairs and let out several cries of pain, I wished I could block the noises out. But it was all over within seconds and, when it was, all was quiet in the house, barring my heavy breathing.

I waited a couple of minutes to make sure she wasn't moving before I went down to check on her. Her body was twisted and her eyes were closed. There was no pulse. There was no life.

There was nothing standing in my way of inheriting all of her wealth.

I knew I had done it.

What I hadn't known was that my eldest son had arranged to visit his grandmother that lunchtime too.

It was as I was standing over my mother's body, feeling a mixture of relief and dread, as well as excitement about my financial future, that Scott knocked on the door. I saw his shape through the frosted glass and knew it was him. I also knew he would have seen my car parked outside and I realised I couldn't just hide in here in the hope that he would go away. I was going to have to let him in and that meant I was going to have to lie to him.

So that's what I did.

Luckily for me, a son will always trust their mother.

THIRTY-SEVEN

SCOTT

THE DAY SHE DIED

'Oh hey. What are you doing here?' I ask Mum when I see her open Grandma's door.

'Er,' she replies before her sentence fails and she just stands and stares at me, totally mute, looking like she's seen a ghost. I mean, sure, I look scruffy because I've just come straight from work and I have got more car grease on my face than usual that I struggled to wipe off beforehand. But apart from that, I'm still her son, so she should easily recognise me.

So why is she looking at me in such a weird way?

'Mum, what's wrong?' I ask her nervously, having never seen her acting this way around me before. But she still doesn't answer, and it's only when I look past her and see what is lying on the floor behind her that I realise what the problem is.

'Grandma?' I cry before pushing past Mum. 'Grandma? Are you okay?'

I can already see that the answer to my question is not a good one based on how my grandmother is lying on the floor.

Her body is twisted and her eyes are closed and she is not responding to my calls.

'What happened?' I cry as I lean down to get a closer look, hoping Mum can fill in the blanks where Grandma clearly can't. But based on the proximity to the staircase, I already have a suspicion that it involves a fall. Then Mum goes and confirms it.

'I just got here before you and found her like this,' she says. When I look back, I see my mother has tears in her eyes. 'She must have fallen down the stairs. I don't know how long she has been here.'

I touch my grandmother's face and she still feels warm, so this accident can't have occurred too long ago. That gives me hope, although that quickly fades when I try to feel for a pulse but can't find one.

'Have you called for an ambulance?' I ask Mum, assuming one is already on the way. But the silence that follows is not promising.

'Mum?' I cry, standing back up and rushing to her. 'Have you called for an ambulance?'

'No, I just got here and I'm confused and...'

My mother's voice trails off, and I realise she is in shock. That's understandable, but it's also not going to help the situation. The only thing that can help it now is having a trained medical professional here who might be able to save my grandma's life.

'I'll call one!' I say as I take out my phone.

'Wait!' Mum cries, surprising me.

'Why?'

Mum stares blankly at me again and she really isn't being of any use to me or her stricken mother in this state, so I ignore her and continue making the call.

'I need an ambulance quickly,' I say breathlessly to the operator who answers. 'We're at number 52 High Cross Road. It's my grandma. I think she's fallen down the stairs and she's not moving, and I can't feel a pulse. You have to be quick. Please!'

As I say all that, I notice Mum standing and staring at what lies between us on the floor, and it's a sobering sight. I'm used to seeing my mother be strong and in control, but right now, she looks totally helpless. Shock and grief is a terrible combination and while I am experiencing it myself, at least adrenaline seems to have kicked in for me. But not for her. She just looks like a zombie.

'No, I don't know CPR!' I scream back at the operator, who has just asked me if I might know how to try and resuscitate somebody who isn't breathing. They tell me they'll talk me through it, and I have no choice but to go along with it, so I put them on speakerphone and then get to work, despite feeling like it's futile. Grandma's neck looks horribly twisted and her eyes carry no light or life.

But what else can I do?

As I follow the instructions, my hands on my grandmother's chest and tears in my eyes, I cannot believe I am here trying to save her life. How did this happen? I only came over here because I'd been feeling guilty lately about not seeing her for a while. I've been so busy with the business and trying to keep things going there that I have neglected my grandmother. My dear grandmother, who has always been so nice to me. The one who used to pick me and my brother up from school whenever my parents couldn't make it. The one who used to feed us both and gave us treats in this house when we played here on weekends. The one who was always there to offer some words of wisdom as we got older and made mistakes of our own as adults. My dear grandmother, who I love but haven't seen enough lately.

Today was supposed to be about me making that right.

I came here for a cup of tea and some cake, and I know she was excited to see me.

But now it's too late.

Now, despite the best efforts of me and the operator on the phone, Grandma is still not breathing, and even when the ambulance arrives and two paramedics enter the house, I already know it's been way too long. When they confirm it, I sink backwards against the wall and cry. It's only when I look up that I see Mum isn't crying. She's talking to one of the paramedics and they are asking her what happened.

She's twirling a finger through her hair with her left hand like I've seen her do many times before.

She does it when she's nervous.

She also does it when she's lying.

As I listen to Mum tell the paramedic that she just got here and found her mother like this, a terrible thought occurs to me.

She isn't telling the truth. She's telling a story. But it's not the real one.

I've been able to tell when Mum is lying since I was twelve. That was the age I was when I first noticed that she always did the same thing when she wasn't telling the truth. My mum always twirled her hair with her right hand. But occasionally, I noticed she twirled it with her left hand. Eventually, I realised there was a pattern to it.

The first time I noticed it was when she told me that my brother wasn't going to school one day because he was ill. She twirled her hair with her left hand as she said it. The next day, I learnt my brother had not been ill but had actually been taken out of school to attend a trial at a local football club. My mother hadn't told me the truth because she knew I would be annoyed or jealous or some combination of the two. That was the day I realised mums could lie to their kids. But the thing I remember the most was the left hand in the hair. It had always been the right hand. So I looked for the pattern again. And I found it again, and again, and again.

I noticed it when Mum lied about all sorts of things, from

big to small. Like why we couldn't have a certain meal for dinner, or why Dad wouldn't be home to tuck us into bed, or any one of a hundred different things a parent says to their child. Sure, most of them are white lies designed to make the parent's life easier, but the key thing was that I had noticed the pattern. Of course, I never told my mum that I had noticed the hair twirling thing. Why would I give away something very useful to me? It would be like a poker player telling the other players at the table to stop making it easy for them. I've never actually told anyone about the hair thing. Not even my brother. I guess I'd always liked having that small advantage over my sibling, even though I love him dearly and tell him almost everything else in life.

The hair twirling thing is my secret.

And right then, as I stood and watched Mum using the left hand instead of the right, I knew it.

Mum was lying about Grandma's death.

There was only one good reason why she would do that.

Because it hadn't been an accident.

She didn't fall down the stairs.

She was pushed.

THIRTY-EIGHT

HAVEN

PRESENT – THE HOTEL

'Liane killed Valerie?' I say, shock and disgust running through my body as I stare at Scott.

'I believe so,' he replies, looking lost.

I can't believe this. It can't be real. Can it?

'No,' I say, shaking my head because I can't accept that I have been so wrong about something that I was so sure of.

'I wish it wasn't true,' Scott says, burying his head in his hands. 'But I just know it is.'

As Scott battles his inner demons, I try to process everything he has just told me. Everything he said about going to his grandmother's house and finding her dead by the stairs. How he tried to save her whilst Liane stood by helplessly. And how he watched as his mother did the one thing she does whenever she is lying.

'But I don't understand,' I say. 'Even if this is true and Liane killed her. Why would she do it?'

'The same reason you thought I killed her,' Scott says. 'Money.'

'But Liane doesn't need money.'

'Everybody needs money. We all just have different reasons for needing it.'

This is all too much to handle, so I turn to the window to see if I can open it to get some fresh air in here. But it's one of those windows like in many hotels where it can't be opened and, suddenly, I feel even more trapped and claustrophobic than I did when I thought Scott was here to hurt me.

'I didn't want it to be true,' Scott goes on as I pace around by the locked window. 'I tried to think of reasons why it wouldn't be. Mum couldn't have killed her own mother. It just seemed impossible. My mum wasn't a murderer. But then I thought about all the things I've heard her say over the years. How much she hated working. How she resented the fact that she would be an old woman before she got to do all the things she wanted to do. How she kept saying she wished she'd win the lottery so life would be easier.'

'Everybody wishes they could win the lottery,' I say. 'It doesn't mean they kill people.'

'But not everybody has a dark side,' Scott says solemnly. 'But my mother does, and now I have seen the true extent of it, I can't do it anymore. I can't live with it, certainly not if other people are confusing her evil for mine.'

Looking at the state of the man sitting before me on the bed, it's clear to see now that he isn't some strong, confident mechanic who was desperate to keep his secrets safe. He's a troubled boy who has grown up under a repressive mother who is the real person in the family capable of bad things.

Scott's biggest problem hasn't been me falsely accusing him of murder.

It's been having a mother like Liane.

Or at least that's what he's leading me to believe. But how do I know this isn't just a ploy on his part to lower my defences?

I guess the only way to find out if this is really true is to call his bluff.

'If you are right and your mum killed Valerie, then we need to go to the police and tell them,' I say. 'We need to get them to arrest and question her.'

'You don't understand,' Scott says, looking up at me with fear in his eyes. 'There's no evidence. My mum will just deny it, but then she'll know that it was me who tipped the police off and she'll hurt me next.'

'She wouldn't hurt her own son,' I say, but Scott shakes his head.

'She killed her mother. There's nobody she won't hurt.'

That chilling sentiment causes me to think about Joel. *Could he be in danger too?*

'Mum has always been prone to dark moods,' Scott tells me. 'My brother and I got used to it growing up. Dad would warn us when we were younger and we would know to try and avoid her until she was feeling better. But it wasn't always possible and, sometimes, she would take her moods out on us.'

'She hurt you?'

'Not physically. But she would shout at us. Tell Joel and me that her life would be easier if she hadn't had us. How expensive we are. How her and Dad would be working their whole lives to pay for us. When I was young, I didn't really get it, but as I got older, I realised how twisted it was for her to say those things to us.'

'But I don't understand. If she's been such a bad mother, why are you and Joel so close to her?' I ask.

'Are we close?' Scott scoffs. 'I moved out of home the first chance I got, taking a job in a mechanic's garage rather than pursuing something else that might have taken more time. I just wanted to earn money so I could get out of that house. As for Joel, he went to Australia, so that's how far he was willing to go to get away from home.'

'But I've sat at the dinner table with you all and there was no sign of any issues,' I say. 'You and Joel always seemed fine around your mother.'

'We do it for Dad,' Scott tells me. 'He's told us that Mum has been seeking help. Professional help. He tells us that she is not a bad person and that she loves us deep down. He tells us that he doesn't want to lose us all. So my brother and I try. But it's all just an act. The truth is, we're both scared of Mum, about the person she is beneath the surface. But I never thought it could get this bad. I never thought she was a killer. Until I saw her that day in Grandma's house.'

I don't know what to say to all of that. If it is true, it is awful. A terrible family history laid bare. It certainly makes my own troubled upbringing seem less of an anomaly now. I always presumed the standard 'two parents, two kids' thing looked perfect from the outside, but it's clear nothing is as it seems behind closed doors. How many other picture-perfect families are like this? How many mothers hate their children? How many children are scared of the people they should trust the most? And how many domestic crimes have been covered up simply because they looked like they were an accident?

'Dad always did his best to ensure family harmony,' Scott says sadly. 'So that's why I tried to keep the family intact. It's why I didn't tell anyone about my suspicions of Mum and it's why I tried to warn you away. I wanted to keep the family together, if only for the sake of me, Dad and Joel. But I also warned you away because I wanted to keep you safe.'

'I understand,' I say, realising how trapped and conflicted Scott has been feeling. 'But this cannot carry on any longer. It has to end. Liane has to pay for what she has done.'

'I just told you, there is no evidence,' Scott cries.

'Then we have to find some,' I say before taking a seat on the bed beside Scott. 'You cannot spend the rest of your life like this. Neither can your brother, or your father. It sounds like you have all suffered enough. If you can't do this for your sake, do it for theirs.'

'I don't know what to do,' Scott admits before burying his head in his hands again, and I am in agreement with him there. I don't know what to do either. But it is clear that something does need to be done and sooner rather than later.

Liane is dangerous and there is no telling what she might be capable of next, especially if I don't give her what she wants and leave her family alone. But I can't leave them, not when I know what danger the other members of this family are in. Poor Frederik, being married to a woman like her for so many years. Poor Scott for having to grow up in a toxic atmosphere in which he knew his mother resented him and longed for a life of financial freedom over responsibility. And poor Joel, my boyfriend, the man I love, for having to experience all of this too.

He's kept it all so well hidden from me, but now I know the family is not as perfect as it seemed on the surface, I realise there were a few warning signs that not all was right. Like in Australia, when Joel would talk about how he was unsure about ever moving back to England. I just thought he was loving life abroad, but what if it was just because it was an escape? Maybe the only thing that would have dragged him back to England was to pay his respects after the death of a loved one. Maybe Liane knew that and that could have also been a part of her motivation when she pushed Valerie down the stairs. Sure, she wanted money and a chance to live the life she felt she had missed out on so far. But what if she also saw a chance to get her son back from the other side of the world, knowing he wouldn't miss the funeral of the grandmother he adored?

'Valerie must have known about Liane's dark side,' I say then. 'She must have known that her own daughter had all these problems and anger in her life.'

'Sure, but she loved her and she never would have imagined her own daughter would hurt her,' Scott says. 'We all thought

Mum was getting better. Dad said so. But now I think the only reason she was getting better was because she had made a plan and she knew that once she had done it, she was going to have everything she ever wanted.'

That sounds awful, as awful as everything else I've heard in the last five minutes.

Scott checks his watch then. 'I need to get back downstairs. Joel is in the bar, and I've been gone way too long.'

He stands then, but I reach out a hand to stop him.

'No,' I say. 'Stay here. I'll call Joel and get him to come to us.'

'What?' Why?'

'Because we all need to talk,' I say firmly. 'And we all need to decide what happens next.'

Scott stares at me as if I'm mad and maybe I am. But there is only one way out of this for us all.

'Liane had a plan to get what she wanted,' I say. 'Now it's time we make a plan to make sure she is punished.'

THIRTY-NINE

LIANE

PRESENT – VALERIE'S HOUSE

There can be a lot of motives for murder. Money is a common one, and that was my main driver. But I'd be lying if I hadn't thought about how my mother's death could be the catalyst for my youngest son to return from Australia and hopefully settle somewhere much closer to home.

I missed Joel terribly when he was overseas and found no solace in messages or occasional video calls. I wanted him closer to me, where he could call around and say hi, share dinner with us, and be a proper part of our lives. I admit that I have not been the best mother to him or his brother. I said some terrible things to both Scott and Joel when they were growing up, things that I regret, but also things that I felt were true at the time. Like how having them had denied me the chance to pursue a career I loved, or pack everything up and just go travelling, or just sleep in past six a.m. on a weekend when I was already exhausted from work. I should never have told my sons that I blamed them for my difficult life, but I did, and that was a mistake. But I have done my best to make up for it over the years, although I can still sense a distance between me and my children. I could still see how Scott was struggling for money with his business yet refused to ever ask us for help or even move back home to save some money himself. And like how Joel picked one of the furthest places on the planet to travel around when Europe was on his doorstep.

Both my boys need their space from me, just like I felt like I needed space from them when they were young. But I have found a way to get Joel back from the other side of the world and now that he has his inheritance money, he intends to stay. That's good. If he had decided to take the money and use it to fund more travelling, I would have got his father to have a quiet conversation with him about how his grandmother would have wanted him to spend her money on something more secure than endless travelling. Frederik would, under my instruction, lead Joel into buying or renting somewhere closer to home, under the pretence that it was 'what his grandmother would have wanted'. Knowing my youngest as well as I do, I know he would have felt guilty if he had gone against what he thought were his grandmother's wishes and so he would have stayed put. But as it turned out, that conversation didn't need to occur because Joel has decided to stay of his own accord.

But there is a catch.

He is staying with *her*.

As long as Haven is on the scene, her and her false accusations against my son remain a problem. She might not have guessed who the real killer in the family is, but she has guessed that there is one. So I am going to have to make a plan to deal with her. Will it be a similar plan to the one I made for my mother? Will this plan also involve murder? I can't see any other option if Haven doesn't go away.

'Joel's here,' Frederik says, looking up from his coffee at the kitchen window, and I turn around to see what he has seen. When I do, I spot our son walking down our driveway towards the door, the bag he packed when he left here with him, but that's all there is. There is no sign of Haven or her bag.

As my husband goes to open the door, I am wondering what has happened to send my son here so soon after he left. But I don't have to wonder for long because it's written all over Joel's face when he enters the kitchen.

He looks sad. Lost. *Single.*

'Are you okay?' I ask him. 'What's happened?'

'She's left me,' Joel mumbles back before Frederik walks in behind him looking sheepish. As I process that shocking but fantastic news, my husband opens the fridge and pulls a couple of beer bottles out.

'It's not too early,' he says, as if reading my mind as he pops off the lids before handing one to his broken-hearted son. 'Not at a time like this.'

Joel takes a long glug of his beer, and Frederik implores me with his eyes to not start talking yet. I stay silent, even though I am itching to ask all the questions I have about why Haven has left. I want to know what she said. Why she said it. And where she has gone now. But I follow my husband's lead and wait until Joel is ready to talk.

'She said she couldn't be with me after everything that had already happened between us all,' Joel explains. 'She said she didn't want me to have to choose her over my family because I'd end up resenting her and it would never work.'

I remain silent because this is all sounding good so far.

'I tried to tell her that we could work it out,' Joel goes on. 'I tried to tell her that we could all apologise and this would get better. But she didn't believe me. She said it would never work. Not when my mother hated her.'

Joel looks at me then and I see tears in his eyes. Does he hate me too?

'I didn't hate Haven,' I say firmly. 'I was just looking out for my family, like I always do.'

'Yeah,' Joel replies quietly before taking another swig of beer.

'I'm sorry, son,' Frederik says then, putting a hand on Joel's shoulder. 'Break-ups are never easy.'

My husband is speaking from experience there because there have been several times during our marriage that we have been on the verge of breaking up. Each of those times was because of me, or at least that was who Frederik blamed it on. He said I could be a nasty person, that there was a side to me that was getting worse, that I brought bad energy into this house. But every time, I managed to talk him around and keep him here, even going to a useless therapist to show how I was 'willing to change'. But now I don't have to worry about him leaving me. He won't want to go anywhere now that we are rich and can do far more fun things than work all day and argue all night.

'I'm sorry too,' I say to Joel. 'I didn't want things to end like this. I just want you to be happy.'

I'm not sure if Joel believes that in this moment or blames me for effectively chasing away his girlfriend, but he doesn't say anything. He just drinks more beer.

'Where is Haven now?' I ask then, eager to know her whereabouts. Hopefully she's long gone, but it's best to get confirmation.

'She said she was going to go back to Australia,' Joel says, which is music to my ears. She couldn't get much further away than that, although I have to be careful not to show my happiness about that fact.

'I see,' is all I say.

There's a bit of an awkward silence then as Joel stares at the label on his beer bottle whilst Frederik and I make eye contact but don't have anything verbal to offer. I figure it won't be long until Joel decides he wants to be alone and goes upstairs to his bedroom and, once that happens, it will likely be a while before he emerges again for a chat. So I decide to say one more thing before that can happen.

'I know it's hard right now, darling, but things will get easier and you will meet someone else one day,' I say, eager to put the thought of another attractive woman in his mind so he forgets about the last one.

'Just take it day by day, son,' Frederik adds, slightly more sensibly than me and my hinting at finding somebody new already.

'Yeah,' Joel says before he finishes his beer and then does what I just predicted he would do. He says he wants to be alone and leaves the kitchen to go to his bedroom.

'I suppose you're happy about this,' Frederik says to me once our son is well out of earshot.

'Happy?' I repeat. 'Happy is an understatement.'

I'm not even going to pretend, not with my husband. So I don't. I just let a large smile spread across my face, one that would mortify my son if he was here to see it, before I head over to the fridge and get a beer for myself.

'Cheers,' I say, raising the bottle towards my husband. 'And so long, Haven. Here's to never seeing you again.'

FORTY

HAVEN

EVENING - VALERIE'S HOUSE

By now, Joel should have done what he was supposed to do and now it's my turn to do what I need to do. That's why I take out the stolen key I still have and put it into the lock on Valerie's front door before going inside the cold, vacant house.

Once inside, I check my phone and see that I have a message from my boyfriend. My boyfriend who just pretended that he is single again.

I did it.

That's the first part of this precarious plan taken care of, so I message Joel straight back with my appreciation.

Well done. It can't have been easy.

That is an understatement, and the truth is, I have no idea how Joel has just done what he has. But he is strong and, more than that, he has a passion for making things right. That's why we go so well together. That's why we are not splitting up at all. But it doesn't hurt that Liane now thinks we have.

Do you still want to do this?

I send that message to Joel and wait for his response, keen to hear and respect his feelings and not just have tunnel vision in my pursuit of bringing his mother to justice.

No going back now.

That's his reply and it tells me all I need to know, so there's only one thing left to say.

I love you.

He replies with the same.

Now it's back to the plan.

As I wander around the house, looking at all the piles of cardboard boxes full of things that Liane has packed away, I cannot believe how she was the killer hiding in plain sight all this time. How I was in this house with her, hiding under the bed, worried that she might catch me because if she did, she would get angry, and shout, and maybe call the police. But the reality was that if she had discovered me hiding here, she most likely would have done something much worse.

Something she had already done before.

Something like take my life without hesitation.

Thankfully, she never got that chance. But it doesn't mean she won't get it in the future. That's why I have to be careful. I'm playing with fire now. Having heard the true depths of craziness that exist in my boyfriend's family, I probably should have just left them all behind. The second Scott told me about his mother and how evil she could be, I could have just bailed and never looked back. Moved on. Got a new boyfriend. One who didn't have a psycho for a mother. Yet here I am, still with my current boyfriend and, right now, still trespassing in his grandmother's home.

I never did like to take the easy option in life.

Because I stayed in that hotel room when Scott confessed to his mother's real personality, and because I saw how broken that poor guy was about it all, I was the one who had to decide what happened next.

So I did.

FORTY-ONE

HAVEN

EARLIER – THE HOTEL

'Hey, it's me,' I say after calling Joel and hearing his voice at the other end of the line.

'Is everything okay?' he asks, and I assume he is still under the impression that I think he was going for a walk when he left this hotel room, rather than what he has really been doing.

'Not really,' I admit. 'Your brother is here.'

'What?' Joel cries.

'I know you were meeting him downstairs in the bar for a drink,' I say. 'But I don't care about that. We've got more important things to deal with. Can you come back to the room so we can talk?'

'Erm, okay,' Joel says, and then I hang up before nodding at Scott.

'He's on his way,' I say, not that Scott replies. He goes into the bathroom and closes the door, and I wonder if he is going to be sick. I certainly feel nauseous after all he has told me, so I could forgive him for feeling the need to vomit. But he emerges a few moments later, still looking pale, but with no evidence of having been sick. I guess he just needed a few moments to compose himself. I hope he got them because the knock at the hotel room door tells us both that Joel is here.

'What's going on?' Joel asks nervously, and he's probably imagining all sorts of awful scenarios. Maybe he's even imagining that me and his older brother are somehow romantically involved with each other and this is the part where I choose Scott over him. But while that would be bad, it's not as bad as what is really going on here.

'You need to sit down and listen to your brother,' I say, taking hold of Joel's hand before nodding. 'It's going to be hard, but it's really important that you do.'

Joel looks at Scott, and while I know their sibling bond is a strong one, it's about to be tested in a way it never has been before. What is about to happen in these next five minutes will push the brothers' relationship to the brink.

'What is this?' Joel asks again.

'Seriously, sit down first,' Scott says, and he takes a seat on the bed before motioning for his brother to join him.

Joel looks at me, and I nod, and then he finally takes a seat. I do the same, sitting in the wooden chair that accompanies the desk in here, and now that we are all comfortable, it's unfortunately time to get uncomfortable.

'Mum killed Grandma,' Scott says to Joel in what must surely be a contender for one of the shortest but craziest sentences ever spoken in human history.

As to be expected, Joel looks like it is the most ludicrous thing he's ever heard. But then Scott explains what he explained to me. About how he was there just after their grandmother had died. How he saw the way his mother was in the immediate aftermath. How he is so certain their mother is lying about what really happened because she is the reason Valerie fell down the stairs. What he doesn't need to go into as much detail about with Joel is their mother's history of behavioural issues and how her anger, frustration and general bitterness at how her life turned out gave her the motivation to kill her own mother to inherit a fortune and change her circumstances forever.

When it's all been said, Joel looks like I must have looked after I heard it.

Except for one very key detail.

He believes it a lot quicker than I did.

'I knew she was hiding something,' Joel says, not crying as I thought he might, but simply staring blankly at the carpeted floor. 'I obviously had no idea it was something as horrible as this, but I could tell there was something she wasn't telling us about Grandma. I just figured it might have been about how the two of them had been arguing recently and they hadn't been on the best of terms before Grandma died. They were always arguing, weren't they?'

Scott nods.

'Mum would moan about something, and Grandma would say that she didn't appreciate how lucky she was, and then Mum would get annoyed,' Joel explains to me. 'It was so common we barely even acknowledged it anymore. I don't think we had a family meal where Mum didn't get annoyed at Grandma for something.'

It's that fact, that sad but relevant experience, that seems to be allowing Joel to see that what his brother has just said is not just possible, but very, very plausible.

'I don't know what we're supposed to do,' Joel says next, showing that while he can believe his mother is capable of murder, he isn't sure we are capable of making sure she is punished for it.

'I have an idea,' I say then, speaking up once I'm sure the siblings have finished their difficult conversation.

Scott and Joel look at me, both brothers needing guidance in this heavy, hard moment. So it's up to me to try and give it to them.

FORTY-TWO

HAVEN

EVENING

As I continue to walk around Valerie's home, looking at the last remnants of her life that haven't yet been shoved into a box destined for either the dump, the charity store or Liane's bank account, I hear a car parking outside.

I freeze before forcing myself into movement again and head down the stairs, rushing towards the door so I can get there before someone else can open it. The door isn't locked. There's nothing stopping the person who has arrived here coming inside and seeing me standing here, where I don't belong.

But I don't bother to try and lock the door to buy myself a little more time. Nor do I consider hiding under a bed like I did the last time I was almost caught here. Instead, I just stand in the hallway, probably in the exact same spot where Valerie landed after she was pushed down the stairs, and I wait to welcome the person who is approaching the front door.

I take a deep breath because this is a crucial moment right here.

This is the part where my plan can succeed or fail.

This is when I find out whether Liane is going to pay for what she did.

Or if I am going to pay for thinking I could ever catch a woman as clever as Liane.

FORTY-THREE

LIANE

I'm setting the dinner table in my family home, a task that I have done countless times over the years. Often, it felt like a chore, like something that had to be done rather than something that I wanted to be done. So many times I was exhausted from work and parenting that the last thing I wanted to do was make the effort to place cutlery down on a table and ensure everyone had the correct place setting for the meal ahead. But tonight is different. Tonight feels special. Tonight feels like an occasion worthy of a family meal.

While I'm down here doing this, my youngest son is upstairs, in his bedroom and licking his metaphorical wounds after the breakdown of his relationship with Haven. I haven't bothered to try and coax him out of there all day, although Frederik had a good idea how we could potentially get him to come out tonight.

'Let's get a Chinese takeaway,' my husband called to suggest to me about an hour ago. 'If that doesn't get Joel out of his bedroom and his bad mood, nothing will.'

I agreed with Frederik because it certainly seemed like it was worth a shot. Having Joel's favourite food for dinner tonight gave us the best chance of getting our youngest son to sit down and talk to us. Or at least sit down and eat while we talked to him. But my husband wasn't done with the suggestions there.

'I'll invite Scott too,' he said. 'I'm sure he won't say no to a takeaway either, and it'll be good for Joel to have his brother around for support. It'll be good for us to have the whole family together for the first time since... well, since she left.'

'I love you,' I had said then in response, simply unable to contain my happiness at how everything was working out. Not only had I successfully managed to get away with murder and make myself rich in the process, the one person who was threatening to ruin all of that was now gone and I was looking forward to eating a tasty takeaway to celebrate that fact.

As the call ended, I couldn't picture how life could get much better. But that was earlier and now, as the front door opens and my nostrils detect the first scent of the delicious food that Frederik has collected on his way home, I realise it is going to get better. Not just because I'm about to be eating all sorts of delicious things, from egg-fried rice and noodles to Peking duck, but because once this meal is over and we've all had a good night's sleep, the fun can begin.

The travel planning. The house-hunting. The new car shopping. Whatever else I want to do with all the money I now have, I'm sure me and my husband are going to get a lot of enjoyment from figuring out ways to spend it.

But before that, I want some bao buns.

'I hope you're hungry,' Frederik says to me as he enters the kitchen, holding up the two big bags of food emblazoned with the logo of our favourite Chinese restaurant.

'Hungry? I'm starving,' I say with a smile before taking the plates out of the oven that I put in earlier so they would be warm when we place our food down on them.

Moments after my husband's grand entrance, I see our eldest son making his own entrance, strolling into the kitchen looking far more clean-cut than he usually does. It's always weird to see him dressed in anything other than oil-stained overalls, but he is wearing a smart T-shirt and jeans combo tonight. He's shaved too. He looks good. Fresh. I make a mental note to make more of an effort with my own appearance now that I have the necessary funds to do so. But I notice one other unusual thing about Scott. He is carrying a cardboard box into the room.

'What's that?' I ask him as he places it down by the table where we will be eating shortly.

'It's a box from Grandma's house,' he says. 'I was over there earlier. It's full of photos that I want to have a look through.'

'How did you get into her house?' I ask before Scott holds up a finger from which a recognisable key is dangling.

'I wondered where that had got to,' I say when I realise it is one of my mum's spare house keys, and the one I noticed had been missing when I was looking for it. 'When did you take that?'

'The other day,' Scott replies casually before tossing me the key, and I place it down on the counter, rolling my eyes at my son's sneakiness.

'You could have just asked to borrow a key,' I say to him. 'You didn't need to take one without telling me.'

'Sorry,' Scott mumbles back before going over to assist his father with all the food.

As the pair of them unpack several containers of noodles, rice and various meats, I figure it's a good time to go and get the one missing member of the family.

I head upstairs before lightly knocking on Joel's bedroom door.

'What?' comes the cry from within.

'Dinner is ready,' I call back.

'Not hungry.'

'We ordered Chinese.'

I count to five before the bedroom door predictably opens and Joel appears, looking like an underground animal coming to the surface for the chance of something to eat.

'How are you feeling?' I ask.

'Rubbish,' comes the curt reply before we go downstairs and join Frederik and Scott at the table.

The generous assortment of food is already laid out, and my eldest son is tucking in, although he pauses respectfully when he sees his brother is here.

'I'm sorry about Haven,' he says simply as his sibling sits down opposite him.

'Thanks,' Joel replies very quietly before the only noise in the room is the sound of cutlery hitting plates.

'We need wine,' I decide before getting up to find a bottle and, when I do, I think about how this is one of the last cheap wines I'll ever be drinking. From here on out, it's only the good stuff.

I pour myself and Frederik a glass before offering our sons one of their own. Scott accepts but Joel declines, though that doesn't stop me pouring one for him anyway.

'It'll make you feel better,' I say to my youngest as I slide the wine glass across the table towards him, and while he looks at it like he doesn't believe that, he eventually picks it up and takes a sip.

'It's been a rough week or so, but things can only get better from here,' I say, raising my glass to the table. 'As long as we all stick together, we'll be fine.'

'I don't know,' Scott says, surprising me.

'What do you mean?' I ask him as Frederik shovels more food into his mouth and Joel pokes his fork at a piece of his meal.

'Don't they say that things happen in threes?' Scott says. 'Good or bad, things tend to occur in patterns of three. So we've had Grandma's death and Joel and Haven splitting up, which makes two. But what's the third going to be?'

I let out a laugh then as I swirl the wine in my glass.

'I don't think you need to worry about nonsense like that,' I say. 'Superstition or myth, or whatever that rule of three thing is. I'm confident that we've got all our bad luck out of the way and things are going to get better from here on out.'

'Bad luck,' Joel says, dropping his knife on his plate. 'Is that what you think all this was?'

'Your grandmother fell down the stairs,' I sadly remind him. 'If that isn't bad luck, I don't know what is.'

'What about Haven?' he asks me then. 'Was she bad luck too?'

'That's not what your mother is saying,' Frederik answers for me, but I don't appreciate that and I make sure to let him know it.

'Maybe I am,' I say, correcting my husband. 'Maybe it was bad luck that you met her. Maybe you could have met some other woman in Australia and things would be very different now. But it doesn't matter. The most important thing is that we are here, together, to enjoy this meal as a family. Because that's all that truly counts, isn't it? Family. And family sticks together at all times.'

I look at each of my family members then, from Joel, to Scott, to Frederik. Then I raise my glass to them all before drinking, realising that I am right about so many things.

This food is as delicious as I expected it to be.

Killing my mother was the best idea I ever had.

And Haven being out of our lives is a very, very good thing.

As I stick my fork into a bao bun, I think about how maybe Scott was right after all.

Things really do happen in threes, don't they?

FORTY-FOUR

HAVEN

'I'm sorry this happened to you,' I say, speaking clearly and calmly. 'You didn't deserve it and nothing I can ever do will make it right. But I promise you that I am going to do my best. I promise that I am going to make your daughter pay for what she did.'

I look around the room I'm standing in as if expecting a response to come from a random direction. But it doesn't. Of course not.

I'm the only person in this room.

I'm the only person in this house.

Still, it was worth saying. I had to say it. I had to let Valerie's spirit know that I am still on her side and always will be. I don't expect her to hear me or understand me or have any kind of reaction to it, but I've said it anyway, if only for my benefit. It's because it has helped me get clear in my mind about what is happening.

More than that, it is to stop me chickening out now it's the pivotal moment.

I take a seat on one of the sofas in this living room, feeling the fabric sag slightly as I sit and thinking about how it would have been perfectly contoured to fit the shape of Valerie. She would have sat here so many times, watching television, having a cup of tea with a friend, and more than anything, talking to her family whenever they visited. I imagine she would have welcomed any of them into her home with open arms whenever they called around. Why wouldn't she? She loved her family. I'm sure she made that clear in life, just like she has made it clear in death.

She left each of her family members a small fortune, ensuring they all inherited money that she worked so hard to make and save over her lifetime. That is something that most people would be extremely grateful for. But it's not enough for everyone. Some people always want more and they want it faster.

They want it all.

Some people like Liane.

Now she thinks she has it all.

But she has no idea how close she is to losing it.

I take out my phone and open the app that I downloaded earlier. I have no idea if it will work as I hope it will, only that I have trusted what I have read online and it all seems legit. But there's only one way to find out if it will work for me right now.

I see a black screen and turn up the volume, holding my breath as I do because this is the moment of truth.

'Can you pass the rice, please?'

I swear my heart skips a beat as I hear Frederik's voice loud and clear through my phone. A moment later, I hear more.

'You really need to try these buns, they're delicious.'

That was Scott.

'I will if you stop eating them all,' replies Joel, and now I know there are at least three of them there, sitting together and clearly enjoying their meal. But where is the fourth member of the family? Where is the one voice I need to hear more than any other?

Where is Liane?

'I knew we should have ordered more,' I suddenly hear her say and I breathe a strong sigh of relief. She is there and like everybody else she is having dinner with, I can hear her voice loud and clear.

That's crucial.

As I keep listening in on the 'private' conversation occurring at a house only fifteen minutes away from the one I'm sitting in, I think about how it was in this room where I sit alone when my plan's success moved from 'possible' to 'likely'. It was in here where, with the help of Scott, I told Frederik what needed to happen next.

I had no idea if it would work.

I had no idea if he would listen to me.

I had no idea if he would choose Liane and love over me and justice.

But I got my answer in the end.

'What's going on here?' Frederik had said as he entered Valerie's house with his eldest son to find me waiting for them both.

'Just calm down, Dad, and listen to what we have to say,' Scott had told his father.

'You shouldn't be in here,' Frederik had said to me. 'How did you get in? We thought you were gone.'

'Dad, please, just let us explain,' Scott had pleaded again and, thankfully, Frederik had fallen quiet long enough for us to try and do just that.

'I'm so sorry to tell you this, but your wife has been lying to you,' I had said as gently as I could. 'She's been lying to us all.'

'What are you talking about?' Frederik had snapped back.

'She's talking about Valerie,' Scott had interjected, and I

was thankful he was there to provide support because it would have been impossible to convince Frederik on my own. 'She's talking about how she died.'

'It wasn't an accident,' I had explained to Frederik. 'She didn't just fall down the stairs. She was pushed. By Liane.'

FORTY-FIVE

HAVEN

THE DAY BEFORE

I'd imagined what Frederik's reaction would be to that statement multiple times in my head, running through every possible scenario I could think of ahead of the difficult conversation in which I called his wife a killer. From him getting angry and denying it, to him breaking down in tears when he realised he was married to a monster, I thought I'd envisioned and prepared for it all. But I wasn't ready for what came next.

'I knew something was wrong,' Frederik had said, looking like a man who had the weight of the world on his shoulders.

Scott and I had shared a look as Frederik had taken a seat, looking sad but also stoic, like this was cutting him up but he was also prepared for it, in a strange way.

'I could see that her mother's death hadn't affected her in a normal way,' he had said. 'She acted sad. But she wasn't. I knew there was something. I just...'

Scott and I waited for him to finish.

'I just never imagined it could be this bad.'

'I'm sorry, Dad,' Scott had said as he took a seat next to his father and offered some support. 'But I was there just after Grandma died. I saw Mum. I saw how she was. I knew something was wrong too.'

Still, Frederik had not got angry and started shouting or got upset and started crying. Instead, he just looked like a man who always knew the day would come when his wife would blow up his family's world.

'I was wrong to accuse Scott,' I had said for clarity then. 'I should have been looking at Liane instead.'

'Now that you are,' Frederik had said, looking up at me. 'What do you intend to happen next?'

'She has to pay for what she has done,' I had replied, wondering if the worn-down husband would choose to defend his wife in that moment. But he just looked at his son.

'How do you plan to do that?' he asked.

'We need your help,' Scott replied, and this was the real moment of truth.

Would Frederik do what we needed him to do? Or would he say no and leave us with nothing?

Would he do the right thing?

Or would he let his wife get away with murder?

Until Frederik spoke again, I had absolutely no idea.

FORTY-SIX

LIANE

EVENING

'I have a feeling things are going to get better for us all,' I say, warming to the theme I was touching on earlier in this family meal. In between then, me and the other diners at this table have commented on all the delicious food we are enjoying, but I am keen to move the conversation back to something a little more substantial than how tasty the king prawns are.

'Your father and I are retiring,' I say to Scott and Joel, hoping they will be as excited about that news as my husband and I are. 'Losing Mum has reminded me that life is short and we can't take our time here for granted, so I think it's important that we try to make the most of whatever time we have left. And I know it's what Mum would have wanted.'

'Did she say that?' Joel asks me as I reach for my glass of wine.

'I'm sorry?'

'Did she ever explicitly say that she wanted you to quit your jobs and enjoy your time?' Joel asks.

'Well, no, not in so many words. But she was my mother, so

of course she wanted me to enjoy life. That is why she has been so generous in leaving us all that money in her will. Why would she do that if she didn't want us to be happy when she was gone?'

'Yeah, I suppose,' Joel replies, but I detect a slight hint of something strange, which puts me on guard a little. It could just be that my youngest son is feeling sad about my desire to make the most of life when he feels like his life isn't in the best place it could be after Haven left him. Perhaps I should have been more delicate about how I phrased what I said. Perhaps the wine I have been enjoying with my meal has already gone to my head and I need to dial it down a little bit. Or perhaps there is nothing to worry about and Joel's question was just a genuine one, coming from a place of curiosity rather than anything else.

'Mum's right. We all need to make the most of our lives,' Scott says then. 'I intend to live life to the full. It's what Grandma would have wanted.'

I smile at my eldest, liking the positive spin he has just added to proceedings.

'I guess we've all got some big decisions to make,' Frederik adds then. 'One thing is for sure, with all this money coming to us, things will never be the same again.'

That sounds very true.

But for some reason, it also sounds very ominous too.

I decide to take another gulp of wine to help me ensure I stay on the more positive side of things.

The food at the table has rapidly diminished and as the sound of cutlery scraping across plates grows quieter, it seems like we are finally achieving something that seemed impossible when we first sat down here.

We are all full.

'Anyone want any more?' I ask as I gesture to the sparse selection of food that remains uneaten between us. But the series of groans and stomach pats give me the answer. I guess we're all done.

'Why don't you boys go and find us a movie we can watch?' Frederik suggests. 'Your mother and I can tidy up here.'

'Are we thinking action or comedy?' Scott asks as he gets up from the table.

'Comedy, definitely,' Joel says as he goes to follow.

'That sounds good to me,' I say, and I smile as I watch my sons leaving the room.

Despite all the struggles recently, what a lovely evening this is turning out to be. And the night is still young.

'How about we open another bottle of wine?' I suggest as Frederik begins carrying the dirty plates to the sink.

'Sure, why not?' he replies, and I'm glad it's not just me who is in the mood for another drink.

As I pull another bottle of white wine from the fridge, I'm expecting Frederik and I to chat wistfully about the exciting future we have as we complete the menial chore of tidying the kitchen. But my husband lets me know that he's seeking something slightly deeper than that.

'How are you coping?' he asks me, causing me to pause before I can unscrew the lid on this latest bottle of wine.

'What?'

'With the grief,' Frederik says as he puts down the dirty plate he was carrying and approaches me. 'I just wanted to check if you're all right or if you're putting on a brave face in front of the boys.'

My husband puts an arm around my shoulder then and I'm touched by his concern. I'd also be lying if I said I wasn't a little annoyed that this sudden bout of sensitivity has taken the shine off my plan to get drunk and be excited about life tonight.

'I'm okay,' I say, making sure to feign some semblance of sadness. 'I mean, I still have some hard moments, but I am okay, I promise.'

I'm not sure I'll ever be technically 'okay' after murdering my mother, but I am still convinced it was the best thing for my family and that thought will surely ease my guilt gradually over the coming years.

'Your mother's passing has hit us all hard, but you especially,' Frederik goes on annoyingly as he guides me back to the table. 'Just sit down for a moment.'

'I'm fine, honestly,' I say but lower myself onto one of the chairs because it seems like the easiest thing to do. If my husband wants a heart-to-heart for a moment, I'll have to give it to him. Maybe this is how the wine has affected him tonight. While it has made me relaxed and carefree, it must have made him reflective and concerned.

'I can see that,' he says next, choosing to stand rather than sit next to me. 'I can see that you are fine and that's what is concerning me the most.'

'What do you mean?'

'I mean, how is it that you can be fine after you killed your own mother?'

I swear it just felt like the world stopped spinning for a second. No, scratch that. It still feels like the world has stopped. Everything is frozen. Time is standing still.

My husband just said I killed my mum.

How the hell does he know that?

All I can do is let out the most nervous laugh I have ever released in my life.

'Wow, you and your dark sense of humour,' I say, slapping my husband on the chest in a playful manner. 'You always know how to make me laugh, but that surprised me, I'll give you that.'

'I'm not joking,' Frederik replies coldly, removing my hand from his chest. 'And I'm certainly not laughing.'

I realise how serious he is now and, suddenly, this moment has got even worse.

'What?' is all I can say next, grateful to be sitting now because my legs feel weak and I would have fallen to the floor if I'd still been standing. That must be why Frederik led me back to the table and this chair. He knew what was coming and he knew how I would react.

'Just admit it,' he says simply.

I twirl my hair with my left hand, and Frederik glares at me.

'I don't know what you want me to admit,' I tell him. 'Seriously, if this is some kind of game, you need to stop because it's not funny now.'

I go to get up then, but Frederik blocks my way.

'There it was again,' he says. 'I can't believe I never noticed it myself in all our years of marriage. But Scott is right. You do twirl your hair with your left hand when you are lying.'

I laugh nervously again. Now what is he talking about?

'You don't realise you do it, do you?' Frederik says, smirking slightly, though he still looks troubled, and deeply so. 'You know you twirl your hair, of course. We all know it. But you don't know that you change hands when you are lying. I didn't even know it. But Scott noticed it. Many years ago, in fact. He figured out when his mother was lying to him. Now I know it, I can figure out when you're lying to me too, and you're lying right now. You did kill your mother, didn't you?'

My hair. My left hand. *My lies.*

I didn't realise I had a tell. If I had, I obviously would have corrected it. But now it's too late for that, so what can I do?

I make a snap decision.

'I did it for us,' I say quickly. 'I did it for the life we can have now. The life we deserve. You can see that, right? You can understand?'

'Oh my god,' Frederik says, taking a small step back from me, but I'm not trying to get away from him anymore. I have to stay and convince him to keep my secret or this is all over. Everything I have done will have been for nothing.

'Think about it. Without my mother's money, we would have both been working for decades. When would we have been able to afford to retire? What if Mum lived into her nineties or even older? She could have outlived us and then all that money she had stashed away would have gone to waste. But now we are free to enjoy it and we can do anything. We can travel the world. We can pursue our hobbies. We can help the boys when they start their own families. We can do anything and we can do it because I only sped up what would have eventually happened anyway. Yes, I killed my mother, but she had lived her life. We still have so much living of our own to do.'

How can that not convince Frederik that what I did was acceptable? How can the life we now have not be better than the one we had before my mum died? He has to understand this, right?

'You're a murderer,' he says sadly, stepping back again. 'You're dangerous and me and the boys are not safe here with you.'

'What? Of course you're safe. I'd never hurt any of you! I love you.'

'You loved your mother and look what you did to her!' Frederik cries, and while I am worried about Scott and Joel hearing this, I need not be when my husband speaks again. 'They both know what you did. We all know.'

That grim revelation prevents me from holding out any hope that my sons can be spared from what I did. But I should have known that anyway, given how Scott was the one who apparently noticed how I behave when I lie.

'What did you think was going to happen?' Frederik asks me. 'That we were just going to live happily ever after with that blood money?'

'It's not blood money. It's my inheritance. It's my right!'

'No, it's murder and that's all it is,' Frederik snaps back, forcing me to go on the offensive.

'So what if it is? What proof have you got? That I twirl my hair with a certain hand when I lie? Now that I know that, I'll stop doing it and what else have you got? What other evidence? None? I thought so. Well then good luck getting the police to listen to this.'

'I don't think I'm going to have any problem getting the police to listen to this,' Frederik replies in a disturbingly simple manner as he walks away from me.

'What do you mean by that?' I ask as I go after him.

'Call the police, Haven,' Frederik says, causing me confusion.

'Haven? Why are you saying her name? She's not here.'

'Isn't she?' Frederik replies.

'Why did you just say Haven's name?' I demand to know as we stand in our kitchen, the remnants of the lovely meal we had just enjoyed still all around us.

'Because she has just heard everything you have said,' Frederik explains, not gleefully, just plainly.

'I don't understand. How could she have heard what I just said?' I ask, looking around the room as if expecting to see Haven hiding somewhere, having eavesdropped on this very private conversation.

'You saw Scott carry this box in here,' Frederik says as he nudges the cardboard box by his feet, the one he brought in before we started our meal. 'But you didn't bother to take a look inside it to see what was in there.'

'I thought it was full of photos,' I reply. 'Old things from my mother's house.'

'Yeah, it is,' Frederik tells me before bending down and reaching into the box. 'But it had something else in it too. *This*.'

At that moment he shows me the phone that had been in there and I recognise the device as belonging to my husband. But why was it hidden inside the box? Why hadn't it just been in his pocket like it should be?

'I'm on a call right now with Haven,' Frederik explains before adding the sucker punch. 'And she has been recording everything we have said.'

Suddenly, heart-stoppingly, I know I am caught. This is the moment I know there is no point fighting.

It's over for me.

And in devastating fashion.

'How could you do this?' I cry as Frederik holds the phone in front of my face, and the only thing that stops me trying to take it from him is knowing he would swipe it away before I got the chance.

'I'm not the bad guy here,' my husband says coldly. 'I'm just trying to make things right. For far too long there has been a toxic part of this family and it has poisoned us all, slowly and gradually over the years.'

'I'm your wife! I'm the mother of your children!'

'Yes, and you're also a murderer.'

That can't be denied. Not after I openly admitted it only a few minutes ago. There I was, thinking that I was doing a good job of convincing Frederik that we could have a great life together now we had Mum's money, when in reality, all I was doing was digging my own grave. I said everything he wanted me to say and there was no taking it back. I could have tried to deny it, to pretend that I was joking, but that wouldn't work. It would have only added further shame and embarrassment to my sinking situation.

So I'm not going to try and take back what I said. I'm too deflated to even attempt it.

Nor am I going to try and change the way my husband looks at me.

I can see all is lost between us and while I can't see my sons at this moment, I know all is lost for me and them too. I can't see Haven either, though I know she is there, still listening in on the call as Frederik holds the phone out of my reach. That's why I can't resist saying one more thing before sitting down and accepting my fate.

'You bitch,' I say loudly and clearly for Haven to hear.

At that, my husband shows me nothing but a smile, but it's not a happy one. It's not one full of joy or hope. It's a sad smile. A smile that says he has won but lost so much in the process.

It's a smile that confirms my worst fears.

Not only have I lost my family now.

I think I'm going to lose my freedom too...

FORTY-SEVEN

HAVEN

FIFTEEN MINUTES LATER

The walk from Valerie's house to Liane's house is a lonely one. But who else could I make it with? Joel is at home with his brother, the pair of them having been sent out of the kitchen by their father just before he initiated his important conversation with his wife. I will be reunited with my boyfriend soon enough, but for now, I am all by myself and it had to be this way.

Somebody had to be elsewhere, making sure that the conversation was being recorded correctly. That somebody was me, and I can happily confirm that everything worked as it should have. The sound of sirens in the distance only makes that belief stronger.

As I keep walking, I send a message to Joel.

Almost there.

He replies straight back.

I love you.

I say the same thing in return before adding something important.

I can hear the police.

I wait to see what he says.

I can hear them too.

If Joel can hear the sirens, that must mean his mother can hear them as well and I wonder how she will be reacting to that. Will she be trying to run? Will she seek to escape and avoid the punishment that is coming her way? Or will she accept her fate and sit calmly in her home, surrounded by her family and all their memories, making the most of her last few moments of freedom before it's gone forever?

As I reach their street and see the house where the crucial conversation took place only fifteen minutes ago, I can't see any sign of Liane leaving. Nor can I see any sign of the police, though the sirens are getting louder and I know they will be here within seconds.

Sure enough, this sleepy suburban street is transformed into a cacophony of chaos a moment later as two marked police cars arrive, swiftly followed by a third, all of them with their blue lights flashing and their headlights aimed directly at the house they are here to visit.

As the cars park and uniformed officers get out, I keep walking towards the same address, eager to get there as quickly as they are, but for a very different reason. While they are here to make an arrest, I am here for something simpler than that.

I am here to give my boyfriend a hug.

I know he is going to need it.

The police officers are just ahead of me, and I watch them as I walk before noticing the front door opening. Frederik appears. He is welcoming the police in, not waiting on them to knock and announce themselves, but actively ensuring not another second is wasted before they make their arrest. That simple sight tells me that he has accepted what has to happen and he will not be offering his wife any of the help I heard her beg him for in the recording. But I already knew he was on board by the fact that he agreed to my plan when I presented it to him as he stood with me and Scott in Valerie's house earlier.

'Take one of these boxes back home with you,' I'd said to Frederik as I gestured to the multitude of stacked boxes full of Valerie's various things. 'Carry it into your house and put it down by the dinner table, right next to where you will be sitting with Liane.'

'Why?' Frederik asked.

'Because inside that box will be your phone and it will be connected to mine,' I had explained. 'We will be on a call together, although neither of us will speak. It will be a secret. Liane will have no idea. But I'll be able to listen in and hear what you are talking about. I'll be able to record every word of it too.'

I'd then explained to Frederik how I had an app that recorded every call on my phone and transcribed the dialogue.

'All you need to do is get Liane talking about what she did to her mother,' I had said. 'She needs to confess to murder. She needs to explain why she did it. Her reasoning. Her motive. How she still wants to get away with it if only you'd agree to stay quiet. If she does all that, we'll have everything we need for the police.'

'You can do it, Dad,' Scott had said then. 'And you need to. For me. For Joel. And for you. We all knew Mum wasn't perfect. But now we know she is a criminal, we can't ignore it.

We have to do the right thing. Mum can get the help she needs in prison. And Grandma can get the justice she deserves too.'

Frederik had taken a little while to answer us both then, but that was understandable. It can't have been easy for a husband to accept a plan to catch his wife for a serious crime. But ultimately, just like his sons, he chose to do the right thing.

'I'll take this box,' he said sadly, and with that, the plan was set.

Now, as I see him stepping aside to allow the police officers into his home, I can see that he is still struggling with the enormity of what has happened. The finality of it all. But it needed to be done. Now it has.

Once I had heard Liane's confession, and checked that my phone had recorded it correctly, I made a call to the police to inform them that there had been a confession to a murder and I had the evidence. I gave them Liane's address and told them that she needed to be arrested before she could try and flee, and that I would meet the officers at the scene and provide them with all the evidence they needed. Now that time has come and I seek out the nearest officer before explaining who I am and handing over my phone that is now a very important part of their investigation. Then I try to get inside to find Joel.

But unsurprisingly, the police aren't keen on anybody else entering the scene, so I am forced to hang back, although not for long. I see Joel step outside, followed by his brother, and it looks like the pair of them are keen to get some fresh air and have a break from that house where so much is happening tonight.

I run towards Joel and wrap my arms around him before squeezing him tightly, and I can feel that he needs such an embrace at this difficult moment. That's why I keep squeezing him and I don't let go until I have told him that I love him and we will get through this together, however hard it may be.

When we separate, I make eye contact with Scott, who lingers nearby and nod my head in his direction, a subtle sign of appreciation for his part in all of this. He nods back too, but there is no need for words between us. We said enough when we were making the plan.

I look back to the house then in time to see Frederik walking out, looking dazed, as if he has just been twelve rounds with a world heavyweight boxer and is now trying to get his bearings again. My heart breaks for him and the path his life has taken, especially how it differed so greatly only a few hours ago. He's gone from thinking that he and his wife were about to retire and travel the world together to learning that the woman he married is a cold, calculating killer and now she is going to prison for the rest of their lives. But bless him, even with all that, he still chose to do the right thing and it's clear where his sons got their strength and bravery from.

They certainly didn't get it from their mother.

And then she appears. Being marched out of the house. Her head bowed and her hands behind her back, her wrists wrapped in cuffs and an officer either side of her. She is being escorted to the nearest police car and, at first, it seems she isn't even going to look up and acknowledge those of us standing by and watching.

But I'm wrong because she does look up.

It's at the last second, but she does raise her head.

When she does, I wonder who she will look at.

Her husband? Her eldest son? Her youngest?

No, she doesn't look at any of them.

Instead, she only looks at one person.

Me.

I'm the last thing she sees before she is bundled into the back of the police car and driven away.

How do I feel about that?

I guess I shouldn't be surprised.

After all, if I didn't know Liane hated me before, I sure know it now.

FORTY-EIGHT

LIANE

How does it feel to not only be caught for a crime, but to have been caught by the people closest to you? To know that none of this would have happened without their help? To know that the only reason you are sitting in a cell surrounded by bars is because your husband and children conspired against you to ensure that this is where you would end up?

It's certainly an awful feeling.

But there's one thing that makes it even worse.

It's that I know I deserve it.

As I contemplate custody and how the rest of my life will look once I've done what my lawyer advises me to do and plead guilty to the charges against me, it would be easy to feel sorry for myself. I've definitely spent a large part of my life feeling that way. It was feeling sorry for myself that led me to do what I did, taking my mother's life simply because I couldn't bear the thought of doing what everyone else manages to do in going to work and having a normal life.

I wanted more.

I got greedy.

Now I am paying the price.

The most galling part of all this is not what I did to my mother. Sure, pushing her down the stairs for my own financial gain was a terrible thing to do and that will form the darkest part of my story when all the journalists tell it in whatever reports they choose to make. But for me, the worst part is that I hurt my family to the point where they saw no choice but to have me arrested, simply so that I couldn't hurt anyone else.

Frederik, Scott and Joel, with *her* help, got me to confess and create the evidence that has allowed the police to have such an airtight case against me. Sure, it hasn't helped that, in my shock and dismay since, I have hardly offered the police a credible story to counteract the accusations and the evidence against me. But really, the damage was done the moment the people I care most about in the world decided that they no longer cared about me.

I can't blame my husband and our sons for what they did.

I can't deny I wasn't shocked to discover it though. Being betrayed and backstabbed by the three people closest to me. The three people I loved the most. The three people I did all of this for. All the time I had spent worrying about Haven and what threat she might have posed to my family, I could never have envisioned that it would be my actual family who brought me down. If only they had stood by me, picked my side, banished Haven to history and gone forward with me instead of her, things could have been so different. We all could have had a better life, a life in which money eased our struggles and there was no shame or scandal brought upon us. Surely that would have been better. But as I sit here in this cell, I know there is only one person it would have been better for. Me. Not them. Because we're different. My husband and our sons can't do the things I did. They can't commit crimes or live with the secret or the guilt or convince themselves that they did a bad thing for a good reason. No, only I am capable of that and it's why they turned against me and picked *her* side instead.

Haven.

My foe.

My arch nemesis.

And sadly, my conqueror.

Having called her a bitch loudly enough for her to hear down the phone, it was off my chest, and I gave up and waited for the police to arrive. Those were a soul-searching and soul-destroying few minutes, but as bad as they were, I didn't want them to end. That's because I knew that when they did, the police would have arrived to arrest me.

Arrive they did, and I was marched very unceremoniously and very shamefully out of my house and into the street, where all my neighbours watched me get put into the back of a police car in handcuffs. Oh, the gossip they must have now. The tales they can tell. The stories they have about their naughty neighbour, the murderer in their midst. I bet I've been the main topic of conversation in every home, coffee shop and restaurant in this town and not for the right reasons. I'd hoped to one day be the talk of the town for being the woman who had all these amazing adventures around the world and who made everybody envious with the exciting life I was leading with my mother's inheritance money. But now I will only ever be known for being a killer, and that's never really the way anyone wants to be remembered.

It's certainly not how I want my boys to remember me.

I hope that in time, they will find the strength to come and visit me in here and give me the opportunity to explain myself. Or if that doesn't work, at least give me the opportunity to apologise. I feel terrible for what I have put my sons through. Their lives won't be easy knowing their mum was a murderer. But they're strong boys and they'll survive. So will Frederik. I know that.

But what about her?

What about the woman who came into my family and blew it up with her accusations and investigations?

If it hadn't been for her, maybe Scott would have been too scared to tell anyone what he knew, that I was the real killer, and maybe all of this could have been avoided.

If it hadn't been for her, I could be sipping cocktails on a beach in the Caribbean right now.

If it hadn't been for Haven, I might have gotten away with murder.

EPILOGUE

HAVEN

How far do you have to go to get away from the sins of the past? Sometimes, even the other side of the world is not far enough. That's the realisation I have come to as I stand on this beach in Western Australia, looking out at the Indian Ocean and contemplating all that has happened to lead me to here. Of course, I'm no stranger to this country and nor is the man standing next to me.

I smile at Joel as we hold hands, the pair of us having returned to the place where we met back when we were just two simple backpackers with no idea how crazy families could really be. It's good to be back, or maybe it's just good to be so far away from home. Either way, we have come to realise that no matter the distance, you carry your emotional baggage with you just as much as the physical kind, and it's unlikely there is anywhere on this planet we could go to forget about Liane and what she did and the impact it has had on all of us.

Beside Joel is his brother and beyond him is their father. All four of us have made this trip to Australia, but we aren't here just for a holiday or a much-needed change of scene. We are here to do something important. Something we hope might bring a little closure to our lives. Most importantly, something that the one person who can't be here would have wanted us to do.

'You should do it,' Scott says as he holds out the urn filled with his grandmother's ashes towards his brother.

Joel lets go of my hand and accepts the urn, although he looks unsure about doing anything else with it.

'How about we do it together?' he suggests, and Scott nods.

Frederik and I share a look before stepping back and allowing the siblings to step closer to the water, the waves that lap at the shore by our feet calm and steady, reminding us of how we aspire to be ourselves.

'Goodbye Grandma,' I hear Joel say.

'Love you,' Scott adds before, together, the brothers take off the lid of the urn.

Then, in one swift move, they allow the contents to flow out, the ashes catching the wind and floating across the water, making this site the final resting place for the wonderful woman who lived a very full life.

Why here? Why spread Valerie's ashes on this beach? The answer to that lies in one of the messages she had sent to me while Joel and I were travelling. Having told Valerie where we had recently visited and having shared several photos with her of the lush location, she had replied to say that it looked incredible. She wasn't wrong. This beach in this part of Australia is truly stunning. The golden sand. The turquoise sea. The clear blue sky. It's picture-perfect, and Valerie said as much. She also said that she wished she had seen such a sight in her lifetime, and while she felt she was unlikely to make the long flight to Australia at her age, she remarked how it would be a wonderful place for her ashes to be scattered one day. That way, she said, it would feel like she had made it and she liked the idea of her final resting place being one far from home, as if to sum up how she liked to do things a little differently in her life.

At the time, her sentiments seemed like nothing more than the whimsical musings of a lovely woman who was sat at her home enjoying some photos from her grandson's girlfriend. But then she died and Liane went to prison for her murder, and in the aftermath, it was obvious that Joel and his family needed a purpose to get them all through the darkest of days. So when I remembered what Valerie had said in her messages to me, I showed them to Frederik, Scott and Joel and then, if they gave their blessing, I proposed a trip. Here we are now, and as we all watch Valerie's ashes sail away on the wind, I can sense that we all feel it was the right thing to be here and do this.

We're a long way from England.

As such, we are a long way from where Liane languishes in a cell.

Joel's mother pled guilty to the charges against her, avoiding a trial and the chance to prolong any pain and suffering on her family's part. She is serving her sentence now, one that likely won't conclude until she has passed away due to old age, a peaceful death that she denied to her own mother. Joel hasn't been to see his mum in prison yet, and I'm not sure that he ever will. That is up to him to decide, as it is Scott's own decision to make too. The same goes for Frederick, all three of these men doing battle with their own internal demons as they try to move on from what has happened and what they have lost along the way.

As for me, I know what is next. Joel and I plan to do some more travelling. With Valerie's money, we can see more of this world, and I think it's vital that we do because if we have learnt one thing in life, it's that the more you see, the more you find the good in it. If I had stayed at home, and if Joel had done the same, our only experience of the world would have been having very dysfunctional families. As it is, we get to learn that there is more to this planet than people who make bad decisions. There is more to life than being hurt by people we love. There is certainly more to the human experience than murder, lies and mistakes.

'I love you,' Joel says to me as he retakes my hand.

'I love you too,' I reply, and we watch the last of the ashes disappear over the ocean before we turn and walk back across the sand to where our hire car is parked.

Suddenly, several grains of sand fly across our faces and we realise Scott has just initiated a beach battle with his brother. It's one that Frederik quickly joins in on too and, within seconds, we are all scooping up sand, scampering around and throwing it before seeking shelter from whoever has the upper hand. It's a harmless, simple situation and anybody watching will likely smile and think about how we seem like a normal family out here having fun. If so, that's good because hopefully we can become a normal family now.

One day, I hope to marry Joel, and we might have a child of our own. If we do, I plan to be a far better mother to my baby than Liane was to him. But it won't be hard to beat her, will it? After all, I just need to avoid killing anybody.

That's easy enough.

Isn't it?

A LETTER FROM DANIEL

Dear Reader,

I want to say a huge thank you for choosing to read *The Girlfriend's Secret*. If you did enjoy it and would like to keep up to date with all my latest Bookouture releases, please sign up at the following link. Your email address will never be shared and you can unsubscribe at any time.

www.bookouture.com/daniel-hurst

I hope you loved *The Girlfriend's Secret*, and if you did, I would be very grateful if you could write an honest review. I'd love to hear what you think!

You can read my free short story, 'The Killer Wife', by signing up to my Bookouture mailing list.

You can also visit my website where you can download a free psychological thriller called *Just One Second* and join my personal weekly newsletter, where you can hear all about my future writing as well as my adventures with my wife, Harriet, and daughter, Penny!

Thank you,

Daniel

KEEP IN TOUCH WITH DANIEL

www.danielhurstbooks.com

facebook.com/danielhurstbooks

instagram.com/danielhurstbooks

PUBLISHING TEAM

Turning a manuscript into a book requires the efforts of many people. The publishing team at Bookouture would like to acknowledge everyone who contributed to this publication.

Audio
Alba Proko
Claire Cowan
Hannah Wilson

Commercial
Lauren Morrissette
Hannah Richmond
Imogen Allport

Data and analysis
Mark Alder
Mohamed Bussuri

Editorial
Natasha Harding
Claire Cowan

Copyeditor
Janette Currie

Proofreader
Lynne Walker

Marketing
Alex Crow
Eleanor Pilcher
Cíara Rosney
Martyna Młynarska

Operations and distribution
Russell Antcliff
Joe Morris
Kiah Tooke

Production
Hannah Snetsinger
Nadia Michael

Publicity
Noelle Holten
Jess Readett
Sarah Hardy

Rights and contracts
Peta Nightingale
Richard King
Saidah Graham
Izzy Beaumont

RAISING READERS

Books Build Bright Futures

Dear Reader,

We'd love your attention for one more page to tell you about the crisis in children's reading, and what we can all do.

Studies have shown that reading for fun is the **single biggest predictor of a child's future life chances** – more than family circumstance, parents' educational background or income. It improves academic results, mental health, wealth, communication skills, ambition and happiness.

The number of children reading for fun is in rapid decline. Young people have a lot of competition for their time, and a worryingly high number do not have a single book at home.

Hachette works extensively with schools, libraries and literacy charities, but here are some ways we can all raise more readers:

- Reading to children for just 10 minutes a day makes a difference
- Don't give up if children aren't regular readers – there will be books for them!

- Visit bookshops and libraries to get recommendations
- Encourage them to listen to audiobooks
- Support school libraries
- Give books as gifts

There's a lot more information about how to encourage children to read on our websites: **www.RaisingReaders.co.uk** and **www.JoinRaisingReaders.com**.

Thank you for reading.

hachette UK